Calvin Durfee

Sketch of the Late Rev. Ebenezer Fitch

First president of Williams College

Calvin Durfee

Sketch of the Late Rev. Ebenezer Fitch
First president of Williams College

ISBN/EAN: 9783337403249

Printed in Europe, USA, Canada, Australia, Japan

Cover: Foto ©Raphael Reischuk / pixelio.de

More available books at **www.hansebooks.com**

SKETCH

OF THE LATE

REV. EBENEZER FITCH, D. D.,

FIRST PRESIDENT OF WILLIAMS COLLEGE.

BY

REV. CALVIN DURFEE.

" In the various relations of life, DR. FITCH was a pattern of kindness and fidelity.'
DR. WOODBRIDGE'S LETTER.

" I have always regarded DR. FITCH as the real founder of this institution."
JUDGE BISHOP'S REMARKS.

BOSTON:

MASSACHUSETTS SABBATH SCHOOL SOCIETY,

DEPOSITORY, 13 CORNHILL.

1865.

Cambridge Press.

DAKIN AND METCALF.

To

DR. SAMUEL SHELDON FITCH, M. D.,

NEW YORK,

A Nephew of President Fitch,

THIS VOLUME

is

Respectfully Dedicated,

by

THE AUTHOR

Williamstown, March 25, 1865.

EXPLANATORY NOTICE.

SHORTLY after the death of PRESIDENT FITCH, which occurred at West Bloomfield, N. Y., his library and manuscripts fell into the hands of his son, the Rev. Charles Fitch, then of Batavia, N. Y., whose house, with all its contents, was soon after consumed by fire. The late Dr. Hyde, of Lee, had been requested to prepare a memoir of DR. FITCH, but soon ascertained that the materials left for such a work were so very scanty that he felt unwilling to make the attempt. The Rev. Dr. Nelson, of Leicester, afterwards commenced, but, for the like reason, soon relinquished, the undertaking. But for the loss of his numerous and exceedingly valuable manuscripts, an extended memoir of his life and services would, unquestionably, have been given to the public years ago.

In preparing this biographical sketch for publication, the author has availed himself of whatever materials he could obtain, and made free use of all the communications he has received. To the late Rev. Dr. Daniel C. Sanders (whose wife was a sister of DR. FITCH); to the late Rev. Charles Fitch; to the Rev. President Day, and to the late Professor Kingsley, of Yale College; to the late President Davis, of Hamilton College; to the Rev. Dr. Walter Clarke; to the late Mrs. Cogswell, of Hartford, for the loan of a large number of letters from DR. FITCH to her husband; to the Rev. Professor Dewey; to the late Dr. Thomas Robbins; to the late James W. Robbins, Esq.; to the Rev. Dr. John Nelson, and to the Rev. Dr. John Woodbridge, — the author

1*

hereby acknowledges himself indebted, and expresses his gratitude for important assistance.

A brief memoir of PRESIDENT FITCH appeared in the " American Quarterly Register," in 1843. This volume is an amplification of that article; and its enlargement and republication, at this time, are mainly owing to a suggestion and to the liberality of Dr. Samuel Sheldon Fitch.

Acceptable aid and encouragement in bringing out this work have likewise been received from two of the author's valued classmates, — David Dudley Field and Josiah William Wheeler.

Whatever of distrust or hesitation might otherwise be felt about giving to the public the results of his additional labor and research is precluded by the many testimonials of approbation received on the appearance of the original article; of which none is more decisive or more highly valued by the author than the following, which he ventures to insert: —

BOSTON, May 4, 1844.

MY DEAR SIR: —

I have received and have perused with great satisfaction your interesting tribute to PRESIDENT FITCH. Accept my thanks for your kindness, in remembering me on this occasion. It is but an act of justice from the living to keep legible the inscriptions on the monuments of the departed worthies; and in this case you have left nothing to be desired.

Very truly your obliged friend,
GEORGE BANCROFT.

REV. CALVIN DURFEE.

CONTENTS.

CHAPTER I.

CHAPTER II.

CHAPTER III.

CHAPTER IV.

CHAPTER V.

CHAPTER VI.

CHAPTER VII.

A DISCOURSE

A SERMON

REV. EBENEZER FITCH, D. D.

CHAPTER I.

BIOGRAPHY USEFUL, AGREEABLE; IF CORRECT, DIFFICULT — DR.
FITCH — HIS EXCELLENT ANCESTRY.

IOGRAPHY is a species of composition which
happily unites the useful with the agreeable.
If written with truth and fidelity, it can hardly
fail to be useful; since it is, as an ancient said
of history, "philosophy speaking by example."
It shows us what qualities we must possess to
be useful and happy. It discloses the trials of
human life; and teaches us how difficulties may be
met, and dangers averted or overcome. It likewise
sets before us the means by which the human character may reach its highest attainments and usefulness.

Nor is it easy to see how the biography of the wise
and good can fail to be agreeable. It introduces us
to the acquaintance of individuals, whose names have
awakened our curiosity, and perhaps our admiration.
It shows those finer and better traits of character
which we could not otherwise narrowly inspect. It

makes us the companions of their toils and trials, their sufferings and joys. It points us to that world where their virtues are matured and their spirits made perfect.

It is painful, however, to think that some great and good men — such as manifest great talents, and exert a wide and salutary influence on society — leave behind them so few materials for the biographer. The traces of their lives and characters soon become dim and obscure. When a few years have swept over their graves, it seems next to impossible, from the few scattered notices now to be found, to delineate with any good degree of accuracy the features of their moral and intellectual character. The good Isis is represented as going forth, wandering and weeping, to gather up the parts and fragments of her murdered and scattered Osiris; fondly yet vainly hoping that she might recover and recombine all the separate parts, and once more view her husband in all his former proportions and beauty. So we often do with the scattered mementos of our departed friends. From a few imperfect sources we attempt to give a faithful history of their lives, and a fac-simile of their moral and intellectual features. *Hic labor, hoc opus est.*

Impressed with sentiments like these, we have undertaken the preparation of a brief biographical sketch of the Rev. EBENEZER FITCH, D. D., for twenty-two years President of Williams College. He possessed a mind of a high order, and for uniformity of deportment, consistency of character, ardor of piety, kindness of feeling, diligence and fidelity in discharging the various duties to which he was called, had but few superiors. It has long been a source of regret to many, that some memorial of this excellent man has not been placed in some permanent form. A simple, uncolored biography of him, even at this late day, and though prepared under great disadvantages, will, we trust, be acceptable to our readers, — especially to the numerous friends and alumni of Williams College. Besides, " some information of this kind is commonly required as a tribute, due to the memory of those who have distinguished themselves in the walks of learning and religion; and may animate others who are devoting their lives to similar pursuits."

President Fitch was a lineal descendant of the Rev. James Fitch, who was born at Bocking, County of Essex, England, December 24, 1622; and came to this country with a brother by the name of Thomas, in 1638. The ancient way of writing the name was *Fytche*. Thomas settled in Norwalk, Ct., and from him, according to Alden, descended the Hon. Thomas Fitch, who was for a number of years Governor of Connecticut. The Rev. James Fitch came to this country when he was sixteen years old. He had already acquired a correct knowledge of the learned languages; but spent seven years in preparing for the ministry, under the private instruction of the Rev. Messrs. Hooker and Stone, of Hartford.

He was first settled in Saybrook, in 1646. In October, 1648, he married Abigail Whitfield, daughter of the Rev. Henry Whitfield, of Guilford. Their children were James, born Aug., 1649; Abigail, Aug., 1650; Elizabeth, Jan., 1652; Hannah, Sept., 1653; Samuel, April, 1655; and Dorothy, 1658. Mrs. Fitch died at Saybrook, Sept., 1659.

In the year 1660, the Rev. James Fitch removed to Norwich with a large part of his congregation. In October, 1664, he married, for his second wife, Priscilla Mason, daughter of Major John Mason, who distinguished himself as a commander of the New England forces against the Pequot Indians. The children of Mr. Fitch by his second wife were, Daniel, born at Norwich, Aug., 1665; John,* Jan., 1667; Jeremiah, Sept., 1670; Jabez, April, 1672; Anna, April, 1675; Nathaniel, Oct., 1679; Joseph, Nov., 1681, and Ebenezer, May, 1683. These fourteen, except the last, lived to have families of children, from whom a numerous posterity has descended.

In his old age, the Rev. James Fitch removed to Lebanon, to live with one of his children, and died there in November, 1702, in the 80th year of his age. †

* John Fitch settled in Windham, and from him descended the Rev. Eleazer T. Fitch, D. D., Professor of Divinity in Yale College.

† The following is the inscription upon his monument, said to have been written by his son, the Rev. Jabez Fitch, of Portsmouth, New Hampshire:

In hoc sepulchro depositæ sunt reliquiæ Viri vere Reverendi Domini JACOBI FITCH, Natus fuit apud Bocking in Comitatu Essexiæ in Anglia, anno Domini 1622, Decembris 24; qui postquam linguis et literis optime

The Rev. James Fitch's oldest son, James, settled in Canterbury, about 1690, and was among its original inhabitants. He built the first framed house and barn in that town. He was one of the brave men who were engaged in the famous Philip's war, in 1675–6; and received a captain's commission before 1680. He was chosen major in 1686. He was a magistrate, or member of the council of the colony, as early as 1683; and continued to be reëlected till 1708 or 9. "He was the first donor to Yale College, who was not of the board of trustees. In October, 1701, he gave the college 637 acres of land in the town of Killingly, and all the glass and nails, which should be necessary to build the college edifice. This benefaction had great influence in procuring the charter, and in encouraging the friends of the college in promoting its interests, and on this account is deserving particular consideration." This James Fitch, Esq.,—he is likewise called Major Fitch, in Trumbull's History of Connecticut,—married Elizabeth ――, Jan., 1676. Their children were James, born (and died within a week after) Jan. 1,

institutus fuisset, in Nov-Angliam venit, ætatis 16, et deinde vitam degit. Harfordiæ per septennium sub institutione virorum celeberrimorum Domini Hooker et Domini Stone. Postea munere pastorali functus est apud Saybrook per annos 14. Illinc, cum ecclesiæ majori parte Norvicum migravit et ibi cæteros vitæ annos transegit in opere evangelico. In senectute vero præ corporis infirmitate necessario cessabat ab opere publico; tandemque recessit liberis apud Lebanon, ubi, semi-anno fere exacto, obdormivit in Jesu, anno 1702, Novembris 18, ætatis suæ 80; vir ingenii acumine, pondere judicii, prudentia, charitate sancta, laboribus, et omnimoda vitæ sanctitate, peritia quoque et vi concionandi, nulli secundus.

2

1677; James, June, 1679; Jedidiah, April, 1681;
Samuel, July, 1683; and Elizabeth, in 1684. Mrs.
Fitch died in October, 1684. Major James Fitch
married, May, 1686, Alice Adams, for his second
wife. Their children were Abigail, born 1687; Ebenezer, 1689; Daniel, 1692; John, 1695; Bridget,
1697; Jerusha, 1699; William, 1701; and Jabez,
1703.

In 1722, Major James Fitch (who died in 1727,
aged 78) gave to his son Jabez, "moved thereto by
love and parental affection," by deed, a piece of land.
This Jabez Fitch married Lydia Gale, in 1722, and
settled on the land which his father gave him. He
became captain, colonel, justice of the peace and
quorum, and was for many years a Judge of Pro-
bate. His children were Jerusha, baptized in 1723;
Alice, afterwards the wife of the Rev. Dr. James
Cogswell, 1725; Perez, 1726; and then there is a
chasm in the records till 1734; when the record of
baptisms commences again, and Lydia is baptized;
Lucy, in 1736; Asahel, in 1738; and Abigail, in
1741. Mrs. Fitch died in 1753. Col. Jabez Fitch
married for his second wife, Elizabeth Darbe, in
1754. Some years afterwards, he buried his second
wife. He was married a third time when about 78
years old. He died in 1784, aged 81. We have un-
questionable authority for stating that Colonel Fitch
was a man of superior talents, unblemished character, devoted piety, and of almost unbounded influence in his native town.

Jabez, son of Colonel Jabez Fitch, was the father of President Fitch. He was born in the parish of Newent, May 23, 1728 or 9; it is uncertain which. According to Norwich records, he was born in 1729; but according to the record of his baptism by the Rev. Mr. Kirkland, he was born in 1728. He married Lydia, daughter of Dea. Ebenezer Huntington, of Norwich, Aug. 22, 1754. Their children were Perez, born Sept. 5, 1755, and died the next day; Ebenezer, the subject of this memoir, Sept. 26, 1756; Lydia, Oct. 9, 1758, and lived ten months; Lydia, June 14, 1760; Abigail, July 24, 1762, and lived just nine months; Jabez Gale, March 20, 1764; Sarah, April 28, 1766; Anna (afterwards the wife of the Rev. Dr. Sanders), Feb. 3, 1768; Chauncey, Jan. 17, 1771; Samuel, March 3, 1773; Lucy, March 24, 1777; and Alice, June 2, 1781. The father of President Fitch did not receive a college education. He was, however, a physician of considerable eminence. Medical students in great numbers resorted to him for instruction. Of his twelve children, three died in infancy; the rest lived to mature age, and became heads of as many families. His five daughters all married men of college education. Two married clergymen; two, physicians; and one a lawyer. One son, Col. Jabez G. Fitch, was for twelve years the United States' Marshal for the district of Vermont, under the entire administrations of Washington and Adams. Another son, Chauncey Fitch, was a physician, and afterwards a judge of a court in Franklin County, Vt.; and Samuel Fitch was a merchant in Burlington.

Mrs. Fitch, the mother of the President, died at Vergennes, Vt. To an intimate friend, President Fitch thus writes: — " My mother left this evil world, I trust for a better, on Monday, April 4, 1803. We have good ground to believe that she has made a happy exchange, — that she has gone to that rest which is prepared for the people of God. Her funeral was attended on Thursday. The Rev. Job Swift was expected to preach; but he and my brother Sanders, as my father was afterwards informed, were both detained on account of sickness. After waiting some hours, the large assembly moved to the court-house, where they sung a funeral anthem. As there was no one present who was willing to offer a prayer on such an occasion, under his heavy affliction and disappointment, my father attempted it. And he states, ' I trust I was enabled to cast my burden on the Lord. By his assistance I was carried through, and felt more able to speak when I closed, than when I began.' " To see a man, who was himself standing on the verge of the eternal world, before a large congregation where a minister was expected to officiate, leading the devotions of the people at the funeral of his own wife, is said to have been a sight so affecting as to draw tears from the eyes of all who were present.

Dr. Fitch, the father of the President, died December 19, 1806, in Sheldon, Vt., at the house of his

son, Dr. Chauncey Fitch, while on a visit. He died
of a lingering consumption. He was a man of eminent piety, and remarkably gifted in prayer. He
made a public profession of religion when a young
man ; and for a number of years held the office of
Deacon in the church of Canterbury. " That religion," writes President Fitch, " which he had so long
professed, afforded him the greatest consolation to
the last. The near approach of death did not appear to terrify or alarm him. He regarded death as
a kind messenger sent by Heaven to release him
from a world of sin and trouble, and convey him to
mansions of eternal rest, there to meet his dear departed friends, and spend an eternity with them in
contemplating the glory, and adoring the perfections
of their God and Saviour."

President Fitch's mother, her father, her only
brother (Dea. Simon Huntington, of Norwich, who
was graduated at Yale College in 1741), and all her
sons, died suddenly ; most of them without an hour's
warning.

We shall now be excused for a brief recapitula-
tion. President Fitch's father was Dr. Jabez Fitch,
and his mother was Lydia Huntington.

His grandfather was Col. Jabez Fitch, and his
grandmother was Lydia Gale.

His great-grandfather was Major James Fitch,
and his great-grandmother was Alice Adams.

His great-great-grandfather was the Rev. James

2*

Fitch, and his great-great-grandmother was Abigail
Whitfield.   ·

President Fitch could truly make the sentiment of
the admired Cowper his own : —

> " My boast is not that I deduce my birth
>   From loins enthroned, and rulers of the earth;
>   But higher far my proud pretensions rise, —
>   The child of parents passed into the skies."

CHAPTER II.

RESIDENT FITCH was the second child of his parents, and was born * Sept. 26, 1756. We must here be pardoned for a brief digression. The Rev. Dr. James Cogswell, who was graduated at Yale College in 1742, and who was for a number of years a minister in Canterbury, married an aunt of President Fitch, whose name was Alice Fitch. Their son, Samuel Cogswell, was about the same age with President Fitch. They were both fitted for college by Dr. Cogswell, were classmates, and very intimate friends. They were admitted members of Yale College in 1773, and were graduated in 1777. Of this Samuel Cogswell further mention will be made in another place.

* It is stated in the history of Berkshire County, and on his tombstone at West Bloomfield, N. Y., that Dr. Fitch was a native of Canterbury, Ct. This is evidently a mistake. That he was brought up in Canterbury, there can be no doubt. But his birth unquestionably occurred in Norwich.

In the early part of his college life, President Fitch commenced keeping a journal, which he continued with a good degree of regularity, until the close of his senior year. For the greater part of the time, he recorded the leading events of every day. It is much to be regretted, however, that during the last three months of this time it is kept in characters which we have been utterly unable to decipher. Our extracts from this journal, though brief, will be more copious and extended than they would be, were it not for the circumstance that scarcely any of his manuscripts are now in existence. His journal commences thus : —

"May 16, 1774. As I have but one life to live, and that extremely short and uncertain, so it becomes me to spend it in a diligent preparation for a future state. And as a careful observance and recollection of God's providential dealings with me may, by the divine blessing, promote my spiritual interest and welfare, by being committed to writing, so I have resolved, now in my youth, to draw up a brief account of my past life, taken partly from my old papers, but chiefly from memory. And oh that, by the free grace of God in Christ Jesus, I may not be permitted to end this journal (provided I should keep it for some time, as is my present intention) without some more perfect knowledge of divine things, and a more sure hope of future happiness, than I now possess."

"I was born at Norwich, Sept. 26, 1756, on Sabbath afternoon ; Sicut parentes aiunt, so my parents have told me. In my infancy I was very weakly, — very subject to convulsion fits. I have often heard my parents say that they had but slender hopes of my living to grow up to years of manhood, for several years after I was born. I continued weakly for some years, though, by degrees,

I outgrew the natural weakness; and my feeble constitution grew
firmer and healthier. I remember nothing remarkable either respecting the awakening of my conscience, or the dealings of Providence with me, until I was ten or eleven years of age. About
that time I was wonderfully preserved from immediate death by
the sudden interposition of divine Providence. I was one day at
the river where some young men were at work, and, while they
were busily engaged, I took a notion to cross the river. It was
not deep. I had frequently observed others as they crossed it.
Having stripped myself, I had gone unobserved by them to the
further side of the river, where there was a narrow place, more
deep and rapid than the rest, which immediately carried me down
into deep water, though the stream still continued so swift as to
prevent my sinking. In this critical juncture, Providence so or-
dered it that one of the persons at work looked up and saw me.
He immediately cried out, when one of them sprang after me,
caught me without much difficulty, and brought me to the shore.
I was not so far gone but that I knew and saw all that transpired ;
though when this young man came, I was just sinking, and must
have drowned inevitably, unseen and unobserved by any, had not
divine Providence interposed for my preservation and deliverance. I remember to have been much terrified and frightened.
But, after I got out of the water, I was more solicitous to conceal it
from my parents (which I did for a year) than to prepare for
that death which I had so narrowly escaped."

The spring following, 1766 or 7, he was exposed
to a similar danger in crossing a brook. The journal then proceeds : —

" I recollect nothing remarkable from this time until the spring
of 1768. Though I remember that during the interim I had more
thoughts of God and eternity than formerly; and was sometimes
much affected at prayers, and when reading religious books. During the spring of this year, my father moved near to the meeting-
house. Soon after this, I was taken dangerously sick ; and my

sickness continued for near a month, and had well-nigh carried me out of the world. But God, of his abundant goodness, was pleased to spare my life and restore me to health again. During this sickness and near approach to death, I had more thoughts of eternal things than I ever remember to have had before ; though I was much of the time inclined to drowsiness. I remember to have had such serious thoughts about death and eternity as to be at times thrown into a flood of tears. In this sickness I had a large swelling in my side, which threatened my life. However, that went away of itself, and by degrees I began to recover my health, though I remained weak for a long time. As my sickness abated, my concern about religion began to wear off. In the fall of this year, my grandfather* died. This event made a deep impression on my mind. After his death, I was brought under greater concern for my soul than ever before. This anxiety for my soul was different from any that I had before experienced, both as to its degree and consequences or attendants." But in what the difference consisted does not appear from his journal.

"June 26. I awoke this morning with but little sense of divine things. Soon afterwards attended prayers in the chapel. Next I retired for secret devotions. This forenoon I heard the president preach from Deut. vi. 4, — *Hear, O Israel ; the Lord our God is one Lord.* Subject, The unity of the Godhead. Near the close of the discourse, the president spoke of that hidden idolatry of the heart, which is so displeasing to God. My conscience accused me of great guilt in this particular ; for I knew myself to be often, yea daily, guilty of this high-handed sin. P. M. the president preached from Rom. vi. 21, — *What fruit had ye then in those things whereof ye are now ashamed? for the end of those things is death.* After meeting, I betook myself to my room, where I had a good opportunity for reading, meditation, and prayer. But oh, how poorly was my heart prepared for such exercises!"

"Sabbath, July 10. My first thoughts this morning were on the importance of spending this day for God. I had some sense

* Probably his grandfather Huntington.

of my responsibilities and obligations to be prepared for a future
state. After prayers in chapel, I engaged in the duties of the
closet with some solemnity and interest. Heard Rev. Mr. Perkins,
of Hartford, preach in Mr. Edwards' meeting-house both parts of
the day: in the morning from that pathetic exclamation of
Thomas, recorded in John xx. 28, — *My Lord, and my God;* in
the afternoon the text was Acts xxiv. 16, — *And herein do I exercise myself, to have always a conscience void of offence toward God,
and toward men.* He was admirably pathetic and copious in manner and expression, elegant in style, and sublime in sentiment.
He showed what was requisite in order to have such a conscience.
First, a knowledge of our duty, and a faithful performance of it.
Second, he offered persuasive motives to induce us to have a conscience thus void of offence. Third, he improved the subject in
offering a variety of excellent remarks. One observation was,
that there are in mortals four springs of action, to wit: appetite,
passion, reason, and conscience. He that acts from appetite, acts
like a brute; he that acts from passion, acts like a child; he that
acts from reason, acts like a man; and he that acts from conscience, acts like a Christian."

" Tuesday, Sept. 13. This day have been busily employed in
making preparation for Commencement. This evening I had an
agreeable interview with my father, who came from home to
attend Commencement, and to visit a brother of his at Stamford,
who is in a low and feeble state of health."

" Wednesday, 14. Attended Commencement exercises, which
were performed to the honor of college, and to the satisfaction of
the audience."

" Thursday, 15. In company with my father and cousin, Samuel Cogswell, went to Stamford; found my uncle weak in body
and dejected in mind, having but little hope of continuing long in
this evil world." Here young Fitch spent a week, enjoying the
company and conversation of his friends in a high degree. In the
course of the next week, " returned to my father's house in Canterbury, and was not a little rejoiced to find my friends all alive

and in good health, having been absent from them about four months."

"January 11, 1775. Close of vacation. This is the first winter vacation in this college. By vote of the corporation it continued three weeks. I remained at college the whole time."

" Friday, April 21. To-day tidings of the battle of Lexington, which is the first engagement with the British troops, arrived at New Haven. This filled the country with alarm, and rendered it impossible for us to pursue our studies to any profit." The next week he returned home. He then visited Providence, R. I.; then went to view the camp in Roxbury and Cambridge, Ms., and returned the first of June to New Haven, and resumed his college studies."

" June 13. I have neglected to keep a regular journal for a short time past. It is now very apparent to me that when I left New Haven last fall, and went to Stamford, falling into company, I lost in some measure that melancholy with which I had been for a long time troubled. For some months I did not attend with regularity to my private devotions. During the winter past, I have enjoyed better health than common, and pursued my studies with a good degree of alacrity and success."

" July 16. Attended public worship in the chapel. In my private devotions I formed some resolutions to live a better life than I have done. As I have always had the ministry in view, I think it high time for me to attend more seriously and diligently to the things of everlasting importance. Considering the infinite importance of being in a state of reconciliation and favor with God, and in an habitual readiness for death; considering, also, the importance of pursuing my studies with diligence, so that I may be prepared to be useful to my fellow-men,— I have determined, by divine assistance, to pursue the following course : —

"As the care of my soul is of the first importance, and yet the most likely to be neglected by me, I will, by the assistance of divine grace, for the future be more attentive to my spiritual welfare. And, 1st. I will have stated seasons for prayer, reading the Scriptures and practical authors, for meditating on what I read, and for self-examination. 2d. I will endeavor to maintain a sober, steady, and regular course of conduct. 3d. In my intercourse with friends, I will make subjects of divinity themes of conversation, in all cases when it can be done to mutual edification. 4th. I will endeavor to read a portion of Scripture every morning and evening. 5th. I will aim so to behave toward my friends, as to merit their regard and esteem; and will strive to banish all envious and jealous thoughts toward them and toward all mankind.

"Respecting my studies, I resolve upon the following plan, which I shall alter, if I find upon trial it will be for my interest:— And 1st. I will rise at four in the morning, and will make it my first business to fix my thoughts upon the duties, trials, and temptations of the day; and will arm my mind with proper resolutions to discharge the duties of the day with diligence and alacrity, and guard as far as I can against temptation to sin, and a waste of time. 2d. I will immediately read some portion of Scripture. 3d. I will then begin the business of the day, and will endeavor to have finished my college studies for the day (having attended to them the evening previous) by noon. 4th. The afternoon shall be devoted to exercise, general reading, and whatever of necessary business may demand my attention. 5th. At the end of every month I will make out a plan of the studies which I propose to pursue the succeeding month. I will then divide these studies into separate portions for each week; and these studies shall be the chief employment of my afternoons."

The careful reader will see that the above plan of study bears some resemblance to that adopted by Dr. Doddridge, as exhibited in his life, which young Fitch speaks of having read about this time.

"Thursday, July 20. This day has been observed throughout these colonies as a day of fasting and prayer. Of the propriety of observing such a day, there can be no doubt, when it is remembered that we are now engaged in a war with England. War was recently proclaimed by Congress. Our army has been for several months before Boston. The result of this contest, God only knows. It may end in the ruin of this whole country. But Heaven grant that it may terminate in the security and firm establishment of civil and religious liberty."

"Sabbath, July 23. Attended public worship in the chapel. Attended to private duties both morning and evening. In the latter exercise my heart was affected with a sense of my sinfulness. I saw clearly my inability to save myself, and how absolutely necessary the merits of Christ are to our salvation. As I have the ministry in view, and am wholly unqualified for such a sacred work, I feel that I ought to leave the pursuit of trifles, and live more to the glory of God. My college course is now half spent, and but little done. By divine assistance, I will double my diligence. The plan of study which I prescribed for myself succeeds much better than I anticipated. This encourages me to pursue it with perseverance."

"Sabbath eve, July 30. During the past week, I have prosecuted my studies with diligence, and I trust with some profit. The plan of studies which I had determined on, I have executed, so as to gain some time for other business."

"Aug. 6. I have not pursued the course of study the week past which I had prescribed for myself. To improve our abilities in writing, our tutor has offered a book to the one who will hand in the best composition."

"Aug. 13. The plan of studies, which I had proposed for myself for this week, I did not accomplish. I had writing on hand, which employed all the hours which were not devoted to classical studies. What I wrote was a trial of genius. I ventured to enter the list with a number of my class, and write for a valuable book offered by our tutor for the best composition. I had the good fortune to have the book assigned to me."

"Tuesday, Sept. 26. To-day I am nineteen years old. I feel

that I am laid under great obligations to devote myself wholly to the service of Him who made me, and has preserved me so long a time; who has favored me with so many undeserved mercies, and such distinguished religious privileges. Time is ever on the wing. It passes away with an amazing rapidity. Therefore, whatsoever I do, must be done with diligence and perseverance ; for death will soon come and close my probation."

"July 24, 1776. Commencement-day. It was a private one. C. Goodrich delivered the Cliosophic oration, — an excellent one, and handsomely delivered. Strong and Lyman, a forensic dispute on the question, ' Whether all religions ought to be tolerated.' The subject was well and ably discussed. Porter, Howe, and Mitchel, spoke a dialogue, and Russell pronounced the Valedictory oration : all well performed. But, to crown all, Mr. Dwight delivered an excellent oration on the present state and future growth and importance of this country.* It was written and delivered in a masterly manner. My collegiate life is fast drawing to a close. One year more, and I shall have done. The time is too short; I wish it were longer."

During the first part of the next month, he was for a few days dangerously sick. On his recovery he writes : " God has been very kind and merciful to me. I deserve to die and perish forever; but he has been pleased hitherto to spare my life. Oh that I might improve his goodness to my salvation ! "

" Aug. 24. Had the pleasure of seeing my dear friend, Samuel Cogswell. He brought me the painful news that college had broken up, on account of the prevalence of the camp distemper."

" Sept. 11. This day my father parted with us, to join our army at New York. The parting was a painful one, as it may be

---

* It is erroneously stated in the life of Dr. Dwight, page 12, that this oration was delivered in 1775. It was delivered in 1776.

the last. But his country calls, and he must go. May God go with him, preserve and return him in safety."

" Sept. 19. This was Fast Day in our State, on account of public calamities."

" Sept. 26. *Dies meus natalis.* Oh, how swift, how fleeting is time! One more year of my life is gone,— gone forever. Oh, what a dream is human life! How does it become me to improve all my time to the best of all purposes,— the service of my Maker! Oh that another year might be allowed me for repentance; and may God in infinite mercy, before the close of this year on which I now enter, make me experimentally acquainted with the way of salvation through Jesus Christ! Oh that I might be firmly and sincerely devoted to his service and glory!"

" Sept. 29. This evening, as my father is absent, I began to pray in the family. Though embarrassed at first, yet I succeeded beyond my expectations. Praise the Lord, O my soul!"

" Oct. 16. Spent the evening in reading Thomson's Seasons. They are delicious food for the mind. They afford not only entertainment, but important lessons of instruction. He wrote in such a masterly manner, with such a feeling sensibility, and such a tender heart, that it would seem as though he must ever engage the attention, awaken the feelings, and draw tears from the eye of the reader. The gloom of nature in the winter is so exquisitely painted, that it cast a deep solemnity over my mind, and called forth the sympathy and compassion of my heart. Especially toward the close, when he touched on the shortness and uncertainty of human life, and all the enjoyments of time, my heart was deeply and tenderly affected. I engaged in my devotional exercises, this evening, with unusual engagedness and concern."

" Oct. 20. This evening my mother related to me her religious experience. I was greatly affected, and rejoiced that I could entertain such a good hope for one who is so dear to me."

" Oct. 22. This morning had a most agreeable interview with my father, who was returning from the army where he has passed some months."

" Nov. 12. Spent the day in study. Felt but little concern for my spiritual welfare. Spoke extempore in the evening on the injustice of the slave-trade."

" Dec. 14. Rose early, and went to see Mr. Manning; found him dead, as I expected." Immediately after the death of this youth, young Fitch went to Canterbury to carry the melancholy tidings to the relatives of the deceased. He then adds under date of

" Dec. 15. Between seven and eight o'clock, I reached home. I had a most agreeable interview with my parents, brothers, and sisters. I came home very unexpectedly to them all. I found the neighbors assembled at our house, and engaged in a religious conference. Two of our family had recently been awakened; and two of our neighbors had been hopefully converted since I left home. Oh that God would carry on his work gloriously, and cause many to return and come to Zion!"

" Dec. 16. This day I designed to return ; but, in compliance with the urgent solicitations of my friends, I concluded to remain till to-morrow. Spent the day mostly in conversation with my friends. I found my dear parents unusually engaged in religion, and I resolved to seek renewing grace with greater diligence. I conversed with my parents about the state of my mind, with great freedom. I had some conversation with my dear sister and brother respecting their salvation, but not near so much as I desired. Oh that God would not leave them, but translate them from the kingdom of darkness into the kingdom of his dear Son!"

" Dec. 17. This forenoon took an affectionate and an affecting adieu of my dear friends. This has been a very affecting visit,— the more so as it was altogether unexpected. Meditated this day on what I had seen and heard. Resolved in the strength of divine grace to maintain a closer walk with God. Had some hope that I should yet be made a monument of redeeming grace, and serve God in the work of the ministry."

" Dec. 18. This day parted with Mr. Manning, who thanked me for what I had done, with tears in his eyes. I have reason to

3*

be thankful that God used me as an instrument of doing an act of kindness to this bereaved and deeply afflicted family. Oh that I had done it from purer motives!"

"Dec. 21. Prayed this evening with some feeling and tenderness. Oh that I might be truly regenerated and devoted to God! I would gladly serve him in the ministry. I know I am entirely unworthy of such a favor. But he sometimes chooses the weak things of this world to accomplish his glorious purposes. Perhaps he may thus use me, which I pray may be the case."

"Jan. 1, 1777. Another year is gone, gone forever, without the possibility of being recalled. One more year is taken from my life; and yet I fear I am without an interest in Christ. I may never see another New-Year's day. May it be my greatest concern to spend all my time to the best of all purposes, — the service of God, and seeking a good hope in Christ, which God grant I may obtain."

"March 12. This evening the sirs (resident graduates) attended our meeting, and we debated the question until eleven o'clock, whether we should admit the ladies to our anniversary exhibition as we did last year. It was finally determined in the negative."

"March 13. Spent the day in making preparation for anniversary. The actors were so displeased that the ladies were not to be admitted, that it was thought best to call a special meeting of the students this evening, and, the question being again put, it was unanimously decided in the affirmative."

"March 17. At one o'clock walked in procession to the chapel, and at two began to act the tragedy before the largest and most splendid audience that we ever before had at anniversary. After the tragedy was concluded, the comedy, called the West Indian, was acted to the great entertainment of the audience, and was deservedly applauded. I was never more agreeably entertained. Every character was remarkably well sustained. After the exhibition, the procession returned as it came."

"March 22. This morning the President (Dr. Daggett) made an address to the students, informing them that on account of the impossibility of supplying college with provisions, it would in a few days be dismissed; and also that he had fully made up his mind to resign the presidency of the college."

"March 28. Parted with my friends, and left New Haven."

Yale College suffered greatly during part of the Revolutionary War. So much was the country exhausted, that it was found difficult at times to furnish the students with their ordinary food in New Haven.*

In the spring of 1777, says the biographer of President Dwight, "college was broken up. The students left New Haven, and pursued their studies, during the summer, under their respective tutors, in places less exposed to the sudden incursions of the enemy." The senior class, of which young Fitch was a member, spent the summer in Wethersfield, under the instruction of Dr. Dwight, who was then a tutor in college. The junior class, under the Rev. Mr. Buckminster, and the sophomore class, under Mr. Baldwin, were in Glastenbury. And the freshman class, under the Rev. Mr. Lewis, was in Farmington. There was no public commencement at Yale College in the fall of that year. At the stated time for commencement, the senior class returned to New Haven and met the government of college, probably in the library room, and there, after listen-

---

* See Prof. Kingsley's Sketch of the History of Yale College, published in the American Quarterly Register for 1835.

ing to the usual "*pro auctoritate mihi commissa,*" &c., received their diplomas.

Just as this work is going into the printer's hands, an educated lady has succeeded in deciphering the hitherto obscure portion of Dr. Fitch's journal; from which a very few extracts will be subjoined.

"Wethersfield, July 20, 1777. Heard Mr. Dwight preach two sermons to-day from Prov. viii. 17, — *I love them that love me, and those who seek me early shall find me.* The sermons were excellent. They were evidently addressed to the graduating class."

"July 22. This has been quarter day. I spoke my dialogue (Messrs. Wright, Lee, and Tracy, spoke the other parts), and the Valedictory Oration, before a very large and splendid audience. I trust I did myself credit. Indeed, all the parts were performed to the entire approbation of the audience." His class consisted of fifty-four, — a much larger one than had ever before graduated at Yale. After their commencement exercises at Wethersfield, the senior class returned to New Haven, and received their degrees."

Wednesday, Sept. 10, 1777, Dr. Fitch writes: "This day I commenced Bachelor of Arts. Our degrees were signed by Mr. Dickinson, and given to us in a private manner; the circumstances of the times preventing a public commencement. Spent the day with classmates and friends. This day closed my academical life. A retrospect of the four years spent in this seat of the Muses raises in my mind alternately the emotions of approval and regret. The confusion of war has frequently interrupted my studies, yet I have the satisfaction to find that I have made some progress in the sciences, though not so great as I could wish, and not near so much as I might, had I been as diligent as I ought to have been. I have ever had the ministry in view, and have flattered myself that before my college life closed, I should have the spiritual qualifications requisite to a minister of the gospel. But, alas! I now find

myself unqualified for that important employment. My parents
are desirous of having me devote my life to the work of the ministry, and I have always been willing to do so; but, unless I am
called by the renewing grace of God, I can never think it my
duty to enter the Christian ministry. What the designs of Heaven
are in relation to me is now an awful uncertainty. Without
renewing grace, I must be wretched in time and through eternity.
No creature can be otherwise than miserable, who, like me, is
separated from the great fountain and perfection of happiness.
May the time soon come, when, by being assimilated to Christ in
temper and conduct, I may be a partaker of his blessedness."

CHAPTER III.

HILE a member of college, President Fitch excelled in every department of study; and was highly esteemed for his blameless and gentlemanly deportment. The life of a diligent and virtuous student in college commonly passes away without any very striking incident or interruption. It is apparent from his journal that from early life he was remarkably conscientious and diligent in the pursuit of learning, and in the cultivation of a well-balanced Christian character. After receiving the honors of his Alma Mater, he passed about two years at New Haven as a resident graduate. During this period, while spending a short time in Canterbury, he was enrolled and drafted as a soldier to go into the army. But he objected, on the ground that he was a member of college, and therefore not liable to do military duty. On the other hand, it was contended that resident

(34)

graduates were not members of college. Mr. Fitch wrote to the President for his opinion on the question. President Stiles wrote back that resident graduates were considered members of college. This released Mr. Fitch from doing military service. A copy of his letter and President Stiles' answer are both preserved among the records of Yale College. Our whole country, it is well known, was at this time in a very unsettled and agitated state. Mr. Fitch spent nearly a year in teaching a select school in Hanover, N. J. In a letter dated Jan. 4, 1780, he says: — " My wages are about eight dollars and fifty cents a month, besides board and horse-keeping. I am about five miles east of Morristown, and eight from the army. Week before last I visited the camp, and had the pleasure of seeing many *old* and some *dear* friends. I found the log-house city on the declivity of a high hill, three miles south of Morristown. There the Connecticut line dwells in tabernacles, like Israel of old. And there the troops of the other States lie, some at a greater and some at a less distance, among the hills, in similar habitations."

Mr. Fitch was admitted to his Master's degree, and appointed a tutor in Yale College in the fall of 1780. This office he resigned in 1783. He then formed a mercantile connection with Henry Daggett, Esq., of New Haven; and, in pursuing the business of the firm, he went to London in June, 1783, and returned the following winter with a large purchase of goods. Mr. Fitch not being acquainted with what are familiarly termed " the tricks in trade," nor with the state and wants of the country at that time, made a most unfortunate purchase. " The goods were of a quality and price, at least many of them, above the wants and habits of the citizens of Connecticut." The consequence was that he involved himself in pecuniary embarrassment, from which he did not extricate himself for a number of years.* In 1786, he was a second time elected to the office of instructor in Yale College, and officiated as senior tutor and librarian till 1791. It is the unanimous testimony of such men as the Rev. Dr. Samuel Shepard, of Lenox, and the Hon. Jeremiah Mason, of Boston, that he was highly respected in that office. At that time the instruction of college was given by the President and tutors. It is not, however, our intention to represent Mr. Fitch, either as a scholar or instructor, as the highest among the high. His native talents and literary acquirements, if not superior to the majority of his associates in office, were unquestionably such as to secure for him a high degree of respect and esteem, so far as he was known. Still he was more distinguished for his moral worth than for his intellectual powers and literary attainments.

* In a letter dated April, 1797, President Fitch writes: " By the assistance of my brother Jabez, I last winter effected a settlement of my old debt with Mr. Daggett. The debt is now reduced to a little more than six hundred dollars, which I can pay in a few years, if my life and health are continued."

President Fitch was probably the subject of renewing grace in early life. Though from some expressions in his journal it would seem that he felt at the time of writing it (in the language of Edwards on the Affections) that " the Spirit was *on* the mind, and not *in* it," yet in after years he referred the date of his conversion to the period preceding his entrance into college, supposing it to have occurred when he was about fifteen years old. While in the field, on a certain day, meditating on his moral state, and contemplating his latter end, he saw himself to be a careless transgressor of the divine law; his heart was overpowered with a sense of sin, and melted into sweet submission to his Maker, who now appeared " long-suffering, abundant in goodness, rich in mercy, and worthy of all love and obedience ;" and to use his own words, " he felt himself drawn to Christ, who now appeared to him altogether lovely." In a letter to the Rev. Dr. James Cogswell, dated Williamstown, June, 1796, he says : " I remember the pious counsels which you gave me and Samuel when we were school-boys together. I retain some of the impressions which your preaching, and particularly your instructions at catechising the children in Canterbury, made upon my mind. By the blessing of God, I trust they were not thrown away."

Mr. Fitch made a public profession of religion while a tutor at New Haven, connecting himself with the college church. In the unpublished diary

4

of President Stiles is the following entry: "May 6, 1787. Lord's day. I attended chapel all day. Dr. Wales preached two sermons on Luke xiv. 22, — *And yet there is room.* Mr. Tutor Fitch and Mr. Tutor Denison were publicly admitted into the college church, and sat down to the Lord's table with us, the sacrament being now administered."

President Fitch was licensed to preach the gospel the same month that he made a public profession of religion. The following is from the record of a meeting of the Association of New Haven West, at the house of the Rev. Mr. Brownson, in Oxford, May 27, 1787: "Mr. Ebenezer Fitch, Tutor in Yale College, having read a sermon before the association, and having given evidence of his church-membership, after examination as to his doctrinal knowledge, and experimental acquaintance with Christianity, was recommended to the churches as a candidate for the evangelical ministry, qualified to preach the gospel, wherever Divine Providence may call him." The ministers present were Rev. Messrs. Mark Leavenworth, Eliphalet Ball, Noah Williston, David Brownson, Jonathan Edwards, Samuel Wales, Alexander Gillet, William Lockwood, and Abraham Fowler.

CHAPTER IV.

LITERARY institution having been commenced in Williamstown, Mass., with an expectation that it would become a college,
Mr. Fitch was urgently solicited to dissolve
his connection with Yale College, and take
charge of it. He was elected to the office
of Preceptor of the academy in Williamstown, October 27, 1790. It was not without much hesitation
and inquiry that he concluded to accept of this ap-
pointment. Early the next year, however, he returned an answer of acceptance, and commenced
teaching a public school there Oct. 26, 1791, " It consisted of two departments,—an academy or gram-
mar school, and English free school, — and under the
direction of Mr. Fitch immediately became prosperous. A considerable number of students re-

sorted to it from Massachusetts and the neighboring States, and some even from Canada."

The reputation and prospective usefulness of the institution strengthened the desire of the trustees and people of Williamstown to effect more perfectly the object in view,—namely, to erect the school into a college. Accordingly a petition, evidently written by President Fitch, and dated at Williamstown, May 22, 1792,—about six months from the opening of the academy,—was signed by William Williams, Theodore Sedgwick, Woodbridge Little, John Bacon, T. J. Skinner, Seth Swift, Daniel Collins, Israel Jones, and David Noble, and presented to the Legislature, praying for an act of incorporation changing the school into a college. This application proved successful, and a college charter was granted by the Legislature June 22, 1793. In August of that year, Mr. Fitch was elected President, and in October following, Williams College was regularly organized by the admission of three small classes. President Fitch now entered upon a theatre of enlarged and responsible action,—one for which, by his learning, talents, and experience in teaching, he was well adapted. In choosing him as the first President of their infant seminary the trustees were eminently united and happy. And that they were neither unwise nor disappointed in their choice cannot be doubted by those who are acquainted with the early history of the college. In his hands, and under his care, it soon acquired celebrity and influence, numbers and usefulness, not surpassed, if equalled, by any sister institution of that period in circumstances no more friendly to success.

In May, 1792, President Fitch was united in marriage to Mrs. Mary Cogswell, the widow of his intimate friend, cousin, and classmate, Samuel Cogswell, Esq., who has been before mentioned. Mrs. Cogswell was the daughter of Major Ebenezer Backus, of Windham, Ct., — a highly intelligent and amiable woman. Previous to her first marriage, she received a matrimonial offer from Samuel Cogswell, Esq., and President Fitch, about the same time. Neither of them was aware that the other had made her such a proposal. She was, however, united to Mr. Cogswell in marriage. Samuel Cogswell, Esq., was a brother of Dr. Mason Fitch Cogswell, of Hartford, the originator and patron of the American Asylum, in that place, for the education of the deaf and dumb. Mr. Cogswell resided in Lansingburg, N. Y., and was accidentally shot dead, on a gunning party, by a friend and fellow-graduate of Yale College, about the time that President Fitch went to Williamstown.

By his marriage, President Fitch became the father of eleven children, ten of whom were sons.*

* The two children left by Mr. Cogswell — Maria, afterward the wife of Major Jonathan Sloan, and James Fitch Cogswell — President Fitch treated as his own, giving the son a public education. He was graduated at Williams College, in 1808. Three of President Fitch's children were born at a birth, May, 1807, two of whom died the June following, of the whooping-cough. One of the three is still living. The children now liv-

Five died young.   The oldest of this number, Ebenezer, had just been admitted a member of college,
and died the night preceding commencement, 1807.
He was a professor of religion, and a youth of great
promise.

After describing some domestic afflictions, in a
letter to a relative, Dr. Fitch adds : —

"But a holy God had a still heavier affliction in store for us.
Alas, must I tell you that my first-born, my Ebenezer, has gone
down to the grave ? So, indeed, it is. In the summer of 1806
he obtained a hope that his heart was renewed by divine grace,
and he afterwards lived like a sincere and devoted Christian. On
the third Sabbath in January, he, with several others, made a
public profession of religion. He was unusually gifted in prayer
and exhortation, and took a modest but active part in the religious
conferences of the young people. Several times in my absence
he prayed in the family with propriety, fervor, and solemnity. It
was usual for him to pray with his brothers in their chamber before retiring to rest, and immediately after they rose in the morning; and we have evidence that he did not neglect secret prayer.
Thus was God, I humbly trust, in infinite mercy preparing him
for the great event which was so near at hand. On Saturday,
the 29th of August, he and several others of his mates were ex-
amined and admitted into college. The next day I preached, and
he was present all day. We had all been ill with a severe influ-
enza. He had it lighter than the rest of the family, and appeared
to be well over it. Sabbath evening he told his mother that he

ing are two sons and the only daughter, Mrs. Lucy Fitch Folsom, whose
husband is an efficient chaplain in the army. Two of Dr. Fitch's sons
were graduated at Williams College, — Mason Cogswell Fitch, in 1815,
who died in 1852 at New Albany, Indiana, a man of wealth and influence;
the Rev. Charles Fitch graduated in 1818, and died in 1864, having filled
up a life of usefulness.

felt unusually well, and retired to rest. Before sunrise on Monday morning I found him afflicted with chills, which were succeeded by fever. I administered some mild remedies, which seemed to remove his fever, and thought little of any danger in his case. I was in the college till noon, and did not till three o'clock take any alarm. I then found his fever high, and called in a physician, who bled him, and all his strength and senses left him at once, and he appeared to be sinking into the arms of death. My pen will not allow me to describe the distressing scene which followed. He expired just after twelve on Wednesday morning of commencement-day. God enabled me to go through the usual exercises of the day; and on Thursday forenoon we attended the funeral, and committed the dear, darling child to the dust. My heart daily bleeds under this sore affliction. But God be praised, — the dear child, I doubt not, is with his Saviour. There, there may he be. I wish not to recall him. Ilis age was fourteen years, six months, and five days. I have now lost a very obedient, affectionate, pious, and promising child. But my loss is his inestimable gain. All is right. All is well. And may God have all the praise."

" The President," says the Rev. Dr. Robbins, who was present on the occasion, " though deeply afflicted, appeared remarkably well. He performed the official duties of Commencement with great correctness and propriety. The funeral of his son was attended the next day, and most of the students remained to sympathize with their deeply afflicted President and his family. When the corpse was deposited in the grave, the bereaved father in a calm and collected tone remarked: " I do not deposit in this grave silver or gold, but my first-born, the beginning of my strength."

The first Commencement of Williams College was on the first Wednesday in Sept., 1795. On the 17th day of June previous, President Fitch was ordained a minister of the gospel, at Williamstown, by the Berkshire Association, with special reference to his station as head of the college. The Rev. Ephraim Judson, of Sheffield, preached the sermon from 2 Timothy iv. 2. *Preach the word.* The Rev. Dr. West, of Stockbridge, gave the charge. And the Rev. Mr. Swift, of Williamstown, gave the right hand of fellowship. In this he remarks: " We rejoice at your readiness to engage in the great work of the gospel ministry, and to make preaching your business at college and other places, so far as your study and business at college will permit."

President Fitch received the honorary degree of Doctor in Divinity, from Harvard University, in September, 1800.

Williams College came into existence in a great measure by the wise and persevering efforts of President Fitch, and prospered greatly under his influence and supervision. From an humble beginning it was raised, chiefly by his instrumentality, to a station of high and acknowledged respectability and usefulness. For a series of years it continued to advance with accelerated progress in usefulness and reputation. Such was the rapidity of its growth, and its almost unexampled prosperity, that at one period of Dr. Fitch's presidency it enrolled upon its

annual catalogue about one hundred and forty students. It was resorted to from all parts of New
England and New York.

The following brief extracts from some of President Fitch's letters will be read, in this connection,
with interest:

"January, 1796. The number of students is increasing so rapidly that we are already in want of another college edifice. We
hope to obtain from the State a grant of a township of land in the
Province of Maine, which, if obtained, will enable us to erect
another building. At present, we have a very likely collection of
young men. They are very studious and orderly, and give us
scarcely any trouble."

Through the influence of the late Dr. West, of
Stockbridge, who was for a number of years Vice
President of Williams College, Dr. Hopkins's System of Divinity was for a time one of the text-
books for the senior class. March, 1797, the President writes: "In future we shall read Doddridge's
Lectures in lieu of Hopkins's System."

The following letter from Dr. West to Dr. Samuel
Hopkins will be read, in this connection, with interest : —

"STOCKBRIDGE, Sept. 19, 1797.

"You spoke in your last of our having prohibited your System
being recited in Williams College. It is true, the trustees have
prohibited it. It was introduced as a classical study without the
order of the corporation. The President introduced it because,
as he told me, he thought it much exceeded anything of the kind
he had seen. But the civilian part of the board, it seems, were

of another opinion. They judged that its being recited would be injurious to the reputation of our new institution. The matter was considerably discussed. The clerical part of the board were all of one mind; and were greatly opposed to its being rejected. But when the vote for its rejection was taken, every hand was up, excepting those of the ministers. Though the world seems to be made for Cæsar, yet we know that Zion's God reigns. The time is not yet come for truth to prevail. But in God's good time it surely will come. The evil one intends to hold the college, but the Lord will support his own cause."

Williams College was early and intimately associated with those views of theology which were advocated and defended by Dr. Samuel Hopkins, who was for twenty-five years a clergyman in Berkshire County. President Fitch, Dr. West, and the Rev. Mr. Collins, and most of the clergy of the county at that day were favorable to Dr. Hopkins's theological views. Williams College was likewise early associated with the cause of missions to the heathen; and its early missionary zeal was the result or fruit of its theology. The one was the precursor of the other. They stood related as cause and effect. And the fundamental truth in its theology and missionary spirit was "disinterested benevolence;" which seems to hold about the same place in the religious world that the attraction of gravitation holds in the natural world; involving the great law of the union and the progress of the race.

"January, 1799. Things go well in our infant seminary. Our number is hardly as large as it was last year. The scarcity of money is one cause of this decrease. Some leave us through mere poverty. But our ambition is to make good scholars, rather than to add to our numbers; and in this we mean not to be outdone by any college in New England. Perseverance in the system we have adopted will eventually give reputation to this institution in the view of all who prefer the useful to the showy."

"Dec. 1799. The college is in a prosperous state. The students continue to be diligent and orderly. We admitted twenty-four freshmen, and have in all eighty-one members of college."

"June, 1801. Our college is prospering. We have admitted forty-five freshmen and nine sophomores this year, and expect to make the number up to sixty before commencement."

"January, 1802. Our freshman class this year is not as large as usual, but we expect it will increase to twenty-five or more. A larger number of them than usual are professors of religion; and I hope will make pious and useful ministers. Notwithstanding the cruel and malicious slanders thrown so profusely of late on the clergy, serious young men, who have the ministry in view, appear not to be disheartened. The great Head of the church will still, I trust, continue a succession of learned and evangelical ministers in his churches in this land. He appears to be interposing remarkably for the increase and encouragement of his church in one place and another; and for the support of the great cause of truth and piety. Amidst all the present dark and threatening appearances, some light shines to console and animate the friends of order, government, and religion. The clergy are now experiencing the trial of 'cruel mocking;' and it will not be surprising if 'scourgings, bonds, imprisonments' and other persecutions should follow, for the trial of their faith and patience. It has been usual for God to suffer his church to sink very low before he appears to deliver and enlarge it. This will probably be eminently the case previously to its last great deliverance and enlargement. I trust that ministers and Christians in general will have grace and strength in proportion to their trials; and have no doubt that true religion will ultimately triumph."

"April, 1802. We have lately had trouble in college. The judgments which we drew up and published to the classes respecting their examination in March, gave offence. Three classes in succession were in a state of insurrection against government. For ten days we had a good deal of difficulty. But the government stood firm, and determined to give up no right. At last, without the loss of a member, we reduced all to due obedience and subordination. Never before had I occasion for so much prudence and firmness; not even in the grand rebellion of 1782 at Yale. Most of the students are now very much ashamed of their late conduct. The present generation of them will not, I apprehend, burn their fingers again. They have found that we will support our authority."

"March, 1803. We have both of our college buildings full of students. Nearly thirty of them are serious professors; and many more of them are such amiable and moral young men that we have strong hopes that they will become truly pious, and make useful and devoted ministers of the gospel. This is truly encouraging, though there is at present no special attention to religion among us."

Nothing occurred to check the prosperity of the college, or cause any serious difficulty or discouragement, for fifteen years. In the summer of 1808 a disturbance took place among the students, concerning which we propose to give some account, nearly in the language of Dr. Chester Dewey.

In the summer just alluded to, the sophomore class became very much dissatisfied with their tutor. At that time the college had but four officers; the President taught the seniors, Professor Olds the juniors, and there was a sophomore and a freshman tutor. The sophomores wished to prevent the continuance of their tutor in college after the next commencement. Accordingly they presented a petition to the President and Trustees, signed by some besides their own class, that their tutor might not be reëlected. This attempt on the part of students to interfere with the government of the college created agitation and disturbance. Those not belonging to the class acknowledged their wrong, and were forgiven. Here the matter rested till after commencement, which passed off pleasantly, — the tutors remaining in office, — and here it was supposed the matter would end. The students returned, hoping that everything would go on in peace.

But Professor Olds felt that the subject must not be left so. He felt that the students must not be allowed to interfere in matters where they had no control. He felt that the tutor had been injured by what the students had said and done. He had persuaded some of the students to make their acknowledgments; and now he wanted those most concerned in getting up the petition to do the same. The Faculty agreed with him in this opinion. When Professor Olds presented the subject to the members of the offending class (now under his instruction), each individual refused to put his name to the paper. The junior class was now in direct opposition to a measure adopted by the Faculty. Recitations were at once suspended in that class, and the whole college was in a state of high excite-

5

ment; and the expulsion of some of those most deeply implicated was seriously apprehended.

When the state of things was reported to the Faculty, the President, after a more careful examination of the case, and obtaining the advice of Judge Daniel Dewey, refused to sustain the Professor and tutors in the attempt to force a confession from the juniors; saying that he had been mistaken in the facts, or he should not have consented to require the proposed acknowledgment. Was this course in the President justifiable? Most certainly.

In the midst of the excitement a committee of the students waited on the President, and begged to inform him of the ground on which they had signed the objectionable petition; that their motive in doing it was to sustain the reputation and usefulness of the college; that before presenting it, they had made it a subject of special prayer; that if the tutor remained, some of the students had made up their minds to leave; that if they had erred, it was in discharging what they deemed to be a duty. This representation and further examination produced a change in the President's course, which was unexpected to the other officers. He said the matter had been managed by Professor Olds, in whom great confidence had been placed, and that he had come to conclusions, and had led them to adopt measures, which the true state of the facts, and the feelings and intentions of the students, did not authorize. He therefore told the Professor that the proposed measure was not called for, and must be given up. Professor Olds now felt that he could no longer hold a respectable standing in the eyes of the students, — that he must be sustained or resign. Without looking at the consequences, the tutors sent in a hasty, inconsiderate resignation ; and in a few hours that of Professor Olds followed.

The college was now left without any officer except the President, and as the vacancies could not be supplied at once, a recess of four weeks was given to the students. At the expiration of that time most of the students returned. Messrs. Chester Dewey, John Nelson, and James W. Robbins were called to the tutorships. The students at once devoted themselves to quiet and profitable study. They pursued an unexceptionable course in all things. Peace, order, and good feeling now ruled.

Professor Olds evidently misjudged on the dishonor of his situation. His keen sensitiveness led him to terminate his connection with Williams College, and afterwards with other institutions, in such a sudden manner that many years of his life were sadly embittered. His mind was of a high order; he was a finished scholar, an excellent linguist, and the whole system of mathematics then taught in our colleges was perfectly at his command.

. But who were among the leading members of the class which Professor Olds considered so refractory, and so unceremoniously abandoned, and which President Fitch, at the peril of being thought wanting in firmness, defended? The late Dr. Justin Edwards, the Rev. S. M. Emerson, Hon. Judge J. H. Hallock, Hon. Judge Daniel Kellogg, Hon. Darius Lyman, Hon. William H. Maynard, the Rev. Luther Rice, one of the early missionaries to the East, and the Rev. John Seward, an early missionary to the West.

"Still from this shock," says President Griffin, "increased by exaggerated reports respecting the extent of the disorders, the college did not recover itself during the administration of Dr. Fitch." And yet he was fully sustained in the course which he pursued by all the Trustees, and by the friends of the college generally. The subsequent history of the class has clearly shown that he was in the right. Time has been his vindicator.

We have given a somewhat full account of this college rupture, because it evidently had no small influence in hastening the President's resignation.

It will be seen, by consulting the Triennial Catalogue, that the largest class that was graduated at Williams College during the presidency of Dr. Fitch, was that of the year 1804. It contained 38. That of 1811 contained 34. Those of 1808, 1809, and 1814 contained 29. Those of 1805 and 1806 contained 26. And the last class that was graduated under Dr. Fitch (that of 1815), contained 24. The following comparison will show the prosperous condition of the college during the administration of Dr. Fitch. During his presidency of twenty-two years the whole number of graduates amounted in all to 460, — an average of about 22 annually. During the six years of Dr. Moore's administration the whole number of graduates was 90, — an average of 15 annually. The fifteen classes which were graduated during the presidency of Dr. Griffin contained in all 311, — an average of 21 annually.

In 1843, the Society of Alumni celebrated the semi-centennial anniversary of the founding of the college. Some of the remarks offered on that occasion by the Hon. C. A. Dewey, who is familiar with the early and later history of the institution, will form a fitting close to this chapter.

" Williams here laid the foundation of a school of an elevated character, and one promising great benefit to the youth in this vicinity. It soon came to be felt that the cause of sound learning and true piety demanded an institution of a more elevated character, — one which might extend its benefits to young men, not in this town merely, but embracing a large circle in an extended region. In the true spirit of our republican institutions, this college was chartered, and by its establishment the facilities of a collegiate education were widely extended. Here benefits of a practical character were secured. It occupied a space remote from other similar institutions; its expenses were of small amount, and easily brought within the compass of all who desired to obtain an education. In truth, it extended the advantages to a large class of young men, who, but for this college, would have been deprived of the advantages of a liberal education; and many who have now a controlling influence in the affairs of National and State governments; many who have adorned the liberal professions; and many who have gone forth to civilize and Christianize the heathen world, would have remained in comparative obscurity but for this institution. The advantages here offered were eagerly

5*

embraced. Young men from every quarter here assembled. Those who would have gone to no other institution were here trained and fitted to be strong pillars in the church and state, — filling the learned professions, occupying the highest stations in our universities and colleges, and honored by seats in our legislative halls.

" Williams College was peculiarly fortunate in its first officers. President Fitch, that good man, who for twenty-two years presided over it, brought to the presidential chair those qualities which gave him extensive influence, and attracted the attention of the friends of learning and science. Uniting the urbane manners of the good-hearted gentleman, highly respectable talents, much and long-continued experience as a teacher, and a heart abounding in love to God and toward his fellow-men, he was beloved of all, and esteemed of all.

" His early associates, as teachers, were men of the highest order. Among them was Jeremiah Day, so long the distinguished head of Yale College; Henry Davis, who afterwards presidep over Middlebury and Hamilton Colleges; Thomas Day and Warren Dutton, both lights of science and literature. And others might with propriety be named in this connection.

" The college had indeed its palmy days, and the evidence of its usefulness soon became apparent. If subsequently there have been days of darkness and depression, they have been shared, it is believed, in common with other similar institutions; for what college has not had its days of darkness and trial?

" The period emphatically one of depression and discouragement as to numbers was that of 1813, 1814, and 1815. The question as to whether a new class was to enter at the new college year was sometimes supposed to depend on the state of things in a private classical school in the little village of Plainfield, and what numbers that good and venerable man and minister, the Rev. Moses Hallock, could send us. There, in retirement, besides his parochial duties, always faithfully performed, this venerable man devoted his time most successfully to the classical education

of young men. Mr. Hallock never forsook us; and in the days of
our greatest need always sent us from his retired cloister a number of goodly youth, and in one instance, I believe, furnished
more than one half of the entire class."

Among the many young men who were fitted for
this college by Mr. Hallock, and who rose to eminence, may be named James Richards, missionary to
Ceylon ; Jonas King, missionary to Greece ; William
Richards, who went as missionary to the Sandwich
Islands, but became Minister of Public Instruction ;
and in this connection the name of William A. Hallock, Secretary of the American Tract Society, ought
not to be omitted. Others have been distinguished
in different professions, among whom are William
H. Maynard, of the New York State Senate, and
founder of the Law School in Hamilton College ;
and Jeremiah H. Hallock, for years a presiding judge
in Ohio.

CHAPTER V.

RESIDENT FITCH ever manifested a deep and lively interest in the spiritual welfare of those who were under his care and instruction. During his presidency, Williams College was repeatedly visited by the special influences of the Holy Spirit; and was made instrumental of preparing many young men for the ministry. More than this: it was honored as the birthplace of American missions to the heathen. It was here that such devoted men as Mills and Hall, James and William Richards, and others of a kindred spirit, received their early training for the missionary work. The repeated revivals of religion, which were enjoyed in that favored college previous to 1815, occurred instrumentally in connection with his faithful and pungent preaching. " At the outset of his career, he took a decided stand against French Infidelity, and had no little influ-

ence in staying its progress. His character for sincerity and kindness added weight to his instructions, and gave him decided advantages as a religious teacher." The only way for the followers of Christ to silence those who oppose and deride Christianity is by a life of consistent and uniform piety. Such a life will do what volumes of argument cannot accomplish. It will not only silence, but it will subdue. It will not merely close the mouth of the scoffer, but it will find its way to his heart. Those who were personally acquainted with Dr. Fitch, daily took knowledge of him, that he had his " conversation in heaven."

To show the views of the founders and early patrons of the college, we shall here introduce an extract from the sermon and charge at Dr. Fitch's ordination : —

" ' Our fathers have done well,' said the Rev. Mr. Judson, in his ordination sermon, ' for they have encouraged the preaching of the word. To promote this good design, they formed themselves into small towns and parishes. In these they built houses for public worship, settled ministers, and usually attended on pulpit instruction. In consequence of this wise regulation, the people of New England have been the most virtuous and enlightened of any in the world. And, what is infinitely more, multitudes are now in glory, praising the ever-living God for the expression of his mercy in giving them a place in this happy land of light.'

" They did more. They erected colleges, with a principal design to diffuse a knowledge of the word. They have appointed divines to preside over them, that the youth might be instructed in religion, as well as in the branches of collegiate science. And it gives us pleasure to see such an one at the head of Williams College, to whom it may be proper, on this occasion, to say a few words in particular.

" Sir, — After the solemnities of this day, in all your steps in the field of science with the young gentlemen under your instruction, you will remember you are a minister of the Lord Jesus Christ, under the most solemn charge to preach his word. Since your residence will be at the college, you will feel yourself under special obligation to instruct the youth in the things of religion. Your advantages for it will be great. You will have the authority of a father; for when we send our sons here, we constitute you their parent. You will have the authority of a president. And in a few moments you will have the authority of a minister of the word. The sacredness of your office will give weight to your example and instruction. With these advantages, and with the Bible in your hand, and its principles in your heart, you have a happy prospect of doing good. You will also be under a charge pressed upon you in the presence of God and the Lord Jesus, and the solemnity of the day of judgment, and the exceedingly important consideration that *the word* is the only thing that will lead youth to a correct knowledge of God, of true virtue and eternal life. You will often reflect that religion is the best qualification they can possess, to prepare them for public usefulness, when they leave this seat of learning, and go forth to be citizens of the world. We, their parents, commit them to your care, above all things wishing you would faithfully instruct them in the things of God."

In his appropriate charge, Dr. West observes : —

" You are called to preside over the seminary of learning in this place. You will remember that to train up youth for the service of Christ in the great work of the ministry, was one principal object which our pious forefathers had in view in the original institution of colleges in this land. Divinity is one important branch of instruction, to which you will be constantly called to attend. We charge you not to teach for doctrine the commandments of men; but that the instructions which you shall from time to time give be drawn from the pure fountain of the word of God. You will remember that the souls of these youth will be, in an important sense, required at your hand. Watch for them, therefore, as one that must give an account."

Theology has always been studied in Williams College, not professionally, but as a part of a liberal education. The Westminster Catechism has always furnished, and does to this day furnish, the regular exercise for the senior class every Saturday forenoon. It was studied in Yale College when Dr. Fitch was there, and by him was transferred to this college. And perhaps no recitations have been more 'highly prized, or remembered with more profit.

The original guardians of Williams College were men of large and enlightened views. Eight of the thirteen original trustees were graduates of Yale College, and most of them were men of distinguished eminence. It was their full intention, from the first, to have an institution of high order, and that should not be inferior to their own Alma Mater, as soon as their means would enable them to accomplish their purposes. Especially did they intend that it should be of a high religious character, and adapted to prepare young men for the service of the church.

In the early days of the college, the number of professors of religion was small; still, even then there were some who maintained a character for consistent and active piety. From the faithful preaching of Dr. Fitch, and from the labor and prayers of the few pious students who were connected with the college, some received impressions which were not effaced till they produced a permanent change. Weekly prayer-meetings were sustained in those early days with great uniformity. There was one held for a number of years every evening in the week at the ringing of the nine-o'clock bell. The meeting was much in the form of family worship. The Scriptures were read, remarks were made, and prayer was offered. " This meeting was sustained uniformly for four years," and, the writer adds, " I believe will be remembered with joy by some in another world."

It was often said, by Dr. Griffin, that revivals of religion began to make their appearance in 1792, in Litchfield and Berkshire counties. Soon after this, revivals began to be enjoyed in the churches generally. The Rev. Mr. Swift, the pastor of the church in Williamstown, was strongly impressed with the belief that he should live to see a revival under his ministrations. In the spring of 1805, this blessing began to be realized, and continued between two and three years. It soon extended to the college. In the spring of 1806, a new impulse was given to the revival in college, by the accession of Samuel J. Mills, whose religious history is familiar, and whose very name is " like ointment poured forth." There were two other young men, classmates of Mills, who

were distinguished for their consistent piety and active usefulness, — namely, James Richards and Rob-
ert C. Robbins. As the result of this early revival,
it is reported that thirteen made a profession of religion, of whom nine became ministers of the gospel.
Another account says, " Besides those who became
members of the church from the classes that were
graduated in 1805, 6, 7, 8, and 9, about seventeen
have since become professors of religion."

This revival, which commenced in 1805, extended
into 1807, so that late in that year Dr. Fitch writes,
" On my return from Sheldon, Vt., the 5th of February last, I found our excellent pastor, the Rev. Mr.
Swift, on his death-bed. I left him in good health, but
found him in a dying state. He lived, however, until the 13th of February, and then left this evil world
to receive the reward of a faithful minister of Jesus.
His death brought great additional labors upon me.
The attention to religion still continued, and I attended meetings and preached often. Since his
death, I have preached about fifty sermons here, besides all the cares and distresses which have attended
me in my family, and discharging all my college
duties. Scarcely time has been left me to take my
necessary food and rest; and I am still involved in
this scene of constant cares and labors, — too much
for any one man to perform."

Gordon Hall became pious in the summer of 1806.
August 1st of that year, he writes: " The revival
still continues, and, to the everlasting joy of saints

and angels, this glorious work has commenced in
college; and a number of students have been hopefully converted." Hall died young; but a life of rare
and consistent devotedness gave him a place in the
highest rank of missionaries. There is another individual still living (1865), who, just before his gradu-
ation in 1806, came decidedly over "on the Lord's
side," and who for a series of years was made extensively instrumental in promoting a spirit of revivals in college, and whose name is held in grateful
recollection by all his surviving pupils, — the Rev. Dr.
Chester Dewey.

" This revival," says Dr. Spring in his life of Mills,
"was among the most signal expressions of favor to
the church." He alludes to the well-known fact that
a zeal for missions to the heathen was here awakened
and developed among a choice circle of young men,
who sustained a weekly prayer-meeting, out of which
grew a foreign missionary association. " I have been
in situations to know," said Dr. Griffin, "that from
the counsels formed in that sacred conclave, or
from the mind of Mills himself, arose the American
Board of Commissioners for Foreign Missions, the
American Bible Society, the United Foreign Missionary Society, and the African School, under the
care of the synod of New York and New Jersey; besides all the impetus given to domestic missions, to
the Colonization Society, and to the general cause
of benevolence in both hemispheres."

It was in the summer of 1806, that " Williams

College began to rise to the sacred distinction of being the birthplace of American Missions" to the heathen. It was in the latter part of July or first of August of this year that the prayer-meeting was held by Mills and his associates under the haystack, where the subject of missions to the heathen was first proposed and prayed over; and was shortly after so far matured that, on the 8th of September, 1808, a Foreign Missionary Society was organized in Williams College,—the first society of the kind in this country,—and formed before the *conversion* of the missionary, Dr. Judson. These incidents, hardly known in their day, and certainly little noticed, are now the acknowledged germ of that great instrumentality in civilizing and christianizing the world, —the American Board of Commissioners for Foreign Missions. The isolated fact that the training which students here received was in the providence of God made influential in the establishment of foreign missions, justly gives to the college the name of " The Missionary College," and, to those who were connected with it and guiding its affairs, a reputation which will be immortal.

In the winter of 1812, another revival commenced in the church in Williamstown, which shortly after extended to the college; but its influence was chiefly confined to the two lower classes. During this season of special refreshing from the presence of the Lord, it is reported that twenty-four were hopefully converted, and a number shortly afterwards. Another report is, that twenty-one were added to the church, of whom thirteen became ministers of the gospel.   Several others felt the power of the revival, and their subsequent lives showed that these impressions or effects were not transient.

If our limits would allow, we should be glad to give the particulars, respecting the conversion of the late Rev. Charles Jenkins, who became a decided and earnest Christian in this revival.   He was afterwards settled in Greenfield, and then in Portland. Some of his sermons are before the public.   But we can only refer our readers to those full accounts of these revivals which are published in the history of the college.

How many a parent's heart might have been gladdened by the reception of such a letter as the following!   Under date of April 20, 1812, Dr. Fitch writes to the late Dr. Hyde, of Lee : —

"We have great reason to bless God that he still continues his good work among us.   Not many instances of deep impression have occurred of late; but some are every week obtaining comfort, and giving hopeful evidence of a work of grace.   We count six or seven hopeful converts among the students, and ten or twelve are deeply impressed.   All who have obtained a hope are members of the sophomore class except one, and I have great satisfaction in informing you that this is your own son.   He had for some time been deeply impressed, and last Friday obtained comfort.   He called on Saturday afternoon, but I was out of my study, and did not see him.   This morning I sent for him, and, Deacon Stratton happening to call in, we both conversed with him.   We think his case one of the most clear and hopeful that

has come to our knowledge in this revival. Very few who give \
satisfactory evidence of a work of grace have come out with
those strong, lively, and ravishing views which sometimes attend
such a work. Still it has clear and indubitable marks of being
a genuine work of the Spirit of God. But in the case of your
son, and indeed in all the others, we must wait to see the fruits.
Two of my own children, C. and L., have been much affected,
but are now comfortable. I hardly dare allow myself to hope
that they are the subjects of a saving change. Professor Dewey
and Deacon S. think they give such evidence as ought to encour-
age a hope. We must wait to see what fruit they produce. We
now have a hope for more than thirty since this revival commenced."

May 8, 1812, Dr. Hyde writes: " I have received
information that Alvan, my eldest son, who is a
member of college, is rejoicing in the Saviour. Dr.
Fitch has given me a short statement of his appearance and manner of conversing, from which I am
led to hope in his case. I rejoice, though with
trembling." *

The last religious meeting of the students in the
spring term of 1812 has been mentioned as one of
uncommon interest. The exciting scenes of the revival had passed away. The strong ties of brother-
ly affection which bound the students to one another
were about to be sundered. The meeting was ten-

* Rev. Alvan Hyde, Jr., was graduated at Williams College in 1815,
and, after studying theology with his father and at Andover, became somewhat distinguished for his successful labors among the early churches in
northern Ohio. He was ordained at Madison, Ohio, Sept. 1, 1819, and
died in Lee August 12, 1824, at the age of 30. While living, he was much
beloved for his consistent piety, highly esteemed as a youthful preacher, and unaffectedly lamented in his early death.

der and interesting throughout. Says one who was present: "It devolved on me to preside. In selecting a hymn to close, my eye chanced to fall on the one beginning, 'Blest be the tie that binds.' I had never seen or heard it before. I succeeded in reading it without much faltering. A tune was named, and singing commenced. About the third verse, brother Burt (the Rev. Federal Burt, now in heaven), who stood by my side, turned away and wept aloud. The next verse was attempted, but voices failed. The place became a Bochim. We hung upon each other, and wept and wept, and so closed the meeting, and went to our rooms to weep alone."

In the spring of 1815, Dr. Fitch concluded to resign the presidency of the college. Just before he left, a third revival of religion commenced. In the course of a few weeks some fifteen were hopefully brought into the kingdom ; and several others received very salutary impressions, whose subsequent lives showed the value of this revival to them. Professor Dewey thinks that the first indications of this revival were in connection with the faithful and earnest preaching of President Fitch, which was at this time uncommonly plain and pungent. It is easier to trace the instrumental than the real causes of religious awakenings. The real causes lie concealed deep in the bosom of Christian experience, and we never gain anything more than occasional glimpses of them. But even the active instru-

mentality of Dr. Fitch in promoting the religious
interests of Williams College will not be openly
and fully disclosed until that day "when the Lord
of hosts shall make up his jewels."

In 1815 the late Dr. Justin Edwards wrote to
President Fitch, asking his opinion about an attempt that was then to be made to establish the
Monthly Concert of Prayer. Dr. Fitch's reply, we
regret to say, we have not been able to obtain. Dr.
Edwards — a former pupil of Dr. Fitch — writes as
follows in favor of a general concert of prayer, to
be · held on the first Monday evening of every
month : "Have we not reason to hope, if such a
union could be formed, that light would break forth
upon us as the morning, and salvation as the noon-
day ?" " Will you have the goodness, dear sir, to
give us your thoughts on this subject, as soon as
convenient ? Should the plan meet the views of
gentlemen of influence in the different parts of
the country, measures will be taken to extend the
information as speedily and widely as possible."
" Could it be extended throughout the United
States, we should then unite with Christians, not
only in this country, but in numerous other countries, in supplicating the greatest blessing which
God can bestow."

CHAPTER VI.

R. FITCH presided over Williams College with a good degree of ability and success, twenty-two years. And with the exception of Dr. Manning, of Brown University, what *first* President ever retained that station for so long a period in this country? He resigned his office in 1815, and immediately accepted an invitation, which he had already received from the Congregational Church and Society in West Bloomfield, N. Y., to become their pastor.

Why did Dr. Fitch resign the presidency of the college? There was a concurrence of circumstances which led him to do it. It is well known that during a few of the last years of his presidency, the institution did not enjoy its usual degree of reputation and prosperity ; notwithstanding Dr. Fitch was aided by experienced and able teachers, and had the counsel and cordial coöperation of a judicious and most excellent prudential committee. It is enough to say that the late Dr. Hyde, of Lee, was a prominent

(68)

member of this committee. Still Dr. Fitch had brought himself to believe, and, it would seem, others were induced to believe, that its isolated and sequestered location presented an insuperable difficulty or hindrance to its growth and prosperity.

This was a leading argument which was afterward employed, — the one, by which all the Trustees but *three* were induced to vote to remove the college to Northampton, provided the consent of the Legislature could be obtained. But if the *location* of the college was the principal cause of its being on the wane during the presidency of Dr. Moore, and for a few years previous, how shall we account for the fact that notwithstanding the many and powerful embarrassments it has had to encounter since that time, it has been, for years past, enjoying a very high, and even uncommon degree of reputation and prosperity? The funds of the institution were small. It was difficult for Dr. Fitch to provide the means of supporting a large and expensive family. Other colleges had come into existence; namely, Middlebury, Burlington, and Union. The consequence was, the number of students in Williams began to decline. Dr. Fitch could not bear to see the child of his affection and nurture droop in his hands; especially he could not endure the thought of having the *cause* of its decline attributed to himself. And some, perhaps, began to feel that it was desirable and expedient to have a younger and more popular man in his place. The time had come when Dr. Fitch thought

the public good and his own personal comfort would
be promoted by his retirement. Besides, it is not to
be concealed that the college had about this time
to encounter an adverse influence, which no institution of the kind can ever meet and prosper. A cur-
rent had begun to set strongly against it in its present
location. An influence, secret and open, was at
work to effect the removal of the college to Northampton, or some town in the old County of Hampshire. Nothing would satisfy a portion of the
community short of removing the college from the
beautiful hills of Berkshire to the valley of the Connecticut. The trustees were divided. The faculty
and many of the students finally came to be in favor
of a removal. Under all these circumstances, the
President judged it expedient to resign.

At a meeting of the President and Trustees of
Williams College, held May 2, 1815, the following
vote was unanimously passed, and may with propriety be here introduced: "Whereas the Rev.
President Fitch has signified to this Board his
determination to resign his office of President at the
ensuing commencement; and whereas, in consequence of the state of the funds, the Corporation
have not been able to give him such a salary as his
situation and the increased expenses of living for
years past have required; therefore Voted, That there
be granted to Rev. President Fitch the sum of twenty-two hundred dollars; one thousand thereof to be
paid him in the month of October next; six hundred

thereof in six months from that time, and the residue
in one year from October next." This sum was
cheerfully paid to Dr. Fitch, as a remuneration for
his long and faithful services as President of the
college, and was particularly gratifying to his feelings. It was esteemed by him an act of generosity,
while the Board considered it an act of justice. It
was both.

As a further indication of the state of public feeling on the subject of the removal of the college, we
here introduce a resolution which was offered by the
Rev. Dr. Packard, of Shelburne, and adopted by the
Board at the very meeting at which Dr. Fitch's resignation was accepted: " That a committee of six
persons be appointed to take into consideration the
removal of the college to some other part of the
Commonwealth; to make all necessary inquiries
which have a bearing on the subject, and report at the
next meeting." It begins to be more clearly manifest why Dr. Fitch resigned the presidency of the
college.

Dr. Fitch was installed pastor of the church in
West Bloomfield, N. Y., in the fall of 1815. In retiring, at the age of sixty, from a life of so much care,
toil, and activity, as his had been, he soon began to
feel and exhibit the enfeebling effects of age. He
continued, however, to discharge the regular and
arduous duties of a pastor for twelve years. He
was then constrained, by reason of age and its consequent infirmities, to withdraw from his stated public labors in the vineyard of his Lord.

Concerning his ministry in that place, Dr. William F. Sheldon writes: " Dr. Fitch was a *faithful* minister, instant in season and out of season, exhorting and warning all, both old and young, to embrace the gospel. He was remarkably punctual in fulfilling all his appointments. Seldom was he absent from the weekly prayer-meetings. Though advanced in age, yet he never seemed to be tired of coming a mile and a half to attend these meetings. For a number of years he was likewise constant in attending a Bible class. Dr. Fitch was a *successful* minister. His uniform Christian conduct was a practical illustration of his preaching. During his ministry among us, we were favored with some precious seasons of refreshing from the presence of the Lord. His preaching was not unfrequently rendered quick and powerful, to the conversion of souls."

But the character and results of his ministry in West Bloomfield shall be given in his own words. On taking leave of his people, Nov. 25, 1827, he delivered a farewell discourse, which has never before been printed entire. We propose to insert the whole of it, — for we are sure it will be read with pleasure and profit, — from Acts xx. 32 : *And now, brethren, I commend you to God, and to the word of his grace, which is able to build you up, and to give you an inheritance among all them who are sanctified.*

" This passage is a part of St. Paul's last solemn and affectionate farewell to the elders of the church in Ephesus. He had before preached in that city and vicinity about three years; and gathered a large church of Jewish and Gentile converts. They retained a strong affection for him as their spiritual father, and he for them as his spiritual children, whom he had begotten through the gospel. Being now on his last journey from Macedonia to Jerusalem, previous to his imprisonment, and not having time to visit the Christians at Ephesus, he sailed by the city and landed at Miletus, a seaport town on the coast, about thirty miles distant. Thence he sent and called to him the elders of the church in Ephesus, that he might give them his last instructions, counsel, and advice, and take his leave of them; for it seemed that it had been revealed to him that he should see them no more. He appeals to them as witnesses of his diligence and faithfulness in preaching the gospel to them, — how he kept back nothing from them that was profitable, but had showed them, and taught them publicly, and from house to house, 'testifying both to the Jews and also to the Greeks repentance towards God and faith towards our Lord Jesus Christ. Wherefore,' said he, 'I take you to record this day, that I am pure from the blood of all men, for I have not shunned to declare unto you all the counsel of God.' 'Take heed therefore,' said the apostle, 'unto yourselves and to all the flock, over which the Holy Ghost hath made you overseers, to feed the church of God, which he hath purchased with his own blood.' Near the close of this solemn farewell address, he introduced the words of our text: 'And now, brethren, I commend you to God, and to the word of his grace, which is able to build you up, and to give you an inheritance among all them who are sanctified.' In improving these words as a subject of discourse on the present occasion, I propose to consider,

" I. The import of this apostolic commendation of the brethren ' to God, and the word of his grace.'

" II. What is implied in ' building them up,' and how this word of God's grace was able, by his blessing, to build them up.

" And, III. How it was able, by the same divine blessing, to give them an inheritance among the sanctified children of God in heaven.

7

" I. The import of this apostolic commendation of the brethren ' to God, and to the word of his grace.' Commending them to God was committing them to his care, protection and blessing,— to the guidance and direction of his Spirit; praying earnestly and fervently that God would take them into his own gracious arms, and ever have them under his own holy keeping, — that he would shield them from danger, from temptation, and from every evil, — that the banner of his covenant love might always be over them, — and that he would guide them by his counsel through all the evils, dangers, snares, temptations, and troubles of this world, and afterward bring them to glory. All this is implied in his commending them to God; and no doubt it was with strong desires and fervent prayers that he thus commended them to the protection and blessing of Almighty God, their heavenly friend, in time and forever. And so, if I had the grace of Paul, would I, my Christian brethren and friends, commend you, on this solemn occasion.

" He commended them also to the word of God's grace. Doubtless he calls it *the word of God's grace*, because it reveals a way in which sinners may be saved by his unmerited favor, through the atoning sacrifice of his Son, and the renewing and sanctifying operation of his Spirit; — a way in which his grace is eminently and wonderfully displayed in the actual salvation of millions of our apostate race. To this pure and precious word of God's grace the apostle commends them.

" 1.   As the sure and infallible rule of faith and practice. In this they learn what they are to believe and to do. In this the character of grace is made known, — a Saviour is revealed, — the terms are plainly stated on which salvation may be obtained, and the consequences of accepting or rejecting this Saviour are most solemnly disclosed. Here, too, their duty to God and their duty to their fellow-men are most clearly stated and strongly enforced. To this rule the apostle commended his brethren as a sure guide to sacred and correct principles and right Christian practice.

"2. He commended them to the word of God's grace as the only sure ground of the Christian's hope. Without a Saviour, there would be no hope for a sinner. Without the shedding of Christ's blood, there could be no remission of sin. Without faith in his blood, Christ to every sinner has died in vain. Has any sinner a good hope of salvation? What are the grounds of that hope? Has he believed in Christ? If he has, then he has repented of his sins, and they are forgiven. They are all washed away in the Saviour's atoning blood. Christ has spoken peace to his soul. He has been renewed by the Holy Spirit. There have been implanted in his soul the fear and love of God, — a hatred and renunciation of sin, and a principle of new and holy obedience. A holy life is the consequence of a new heart, — a life devoted to the service of God. Does the believing, hoping sinner desire to know that he has good grounds for his hope? He must go to the word of God, and compare his heart and life with this rule. 'To the law and to the testimony.' If he finds the evidence to be good that he is a child of God and an heir of heaven, he may then hope 'with joy unspeakable and full of glory.'

"3. The apostle commends his brethren to the word of God's grace as the great source of Christian consolation. He who has a good hope that he is a Christian may go to the word of God, and appropriate to himself all 'the great and precious promises' he finds there. From these he may drink in abundant consolation under his severest trials, and heaviest afflictions. This well of consolation is full of living water. Christians can never draw it dry. And the language of the Saviour to them is, 'Drink, O friends, yea, drink abundantly, O beloved.' To this 'word of God's grace,' then, on this and on other accounts which I have not time now to mention, I would, my Christian brethren and friends, earnestly and devoutly commend you all.

"II. What is implied in building them up; and how this word of God's grace was able, by his blessing, to build them up.

"The church is the building of God. It is his workmanship, his edifice, his temple. He laid the foundation, which is Christ

Jesus, his Son; and he has fitted, prepared, polished, and put into this building every stone of which it is composed. This edifice has been in building almost six thousand years, and is not yet completed. Many more stones are to be laid, before the top-stone will be brought forth with shouting. The word of God is the great means or instrument which he uses in carrying on his work on this building. In allusion to this, the expression 'building up' and similar expressions are often used in the Scriptures, and applied to the church, or a body of believers. To build them up is to establish them in the belief and practice of the gospel, — to make them stable, consistent, growing Christians. sound and steadfast in the faith, — not carried about by every wind of doctrine, not soon shaken in mind by dangerous errors and heresies that may be propagated among them; but firm and unwavering in their belief of the great doctrines of the gospel, and able and ready, if need be, 'earnestly to contend for the faith once delivered to the saints.' Building them up implies also their firm establishment in the regular, consistent, and uniform practice of Christian duties; in a word, that they may be exemplary, growing Christians, increasing in knowledge and grace, and adorning the holy religion they profess, both by steadfastly adhering to its doctrines, and uniformly practising its duties. All this, the word of God, by the enlightening, quickening, sanctifying influence of his Spirit, is able to effect, and is the great appointed means of effecting, in their hearts and lives. We are to consider,

" III. How, or in what sense, the word of God's grace is able also, through the same divine influence, to give Christians at last a blessed inheritance among the sanctified children of God in heaven. The Psalmist says, ' The law of the Lord is perfect, con-verting the soul.' In the hands of the Spirit, it is the means or in-strument of the sinner's conversion, and, in the same way, the means or instrument of his progressive sanctification. It is the means of his growth in knowledge and holiness, and of his prep-aration for heaven. God's word is pure, and exerts a purifying influence on the heart. It detects and exposes the secret sins

which are harbored there. It opens the fountain of indwelling
corruption, and brings to light the hidden things of darkness.
It is a refiner and a purifier. It is like the fire and hammer to
break in pieces the flinty hearts, and cause godly sorrow for sin to
spring up there, and tears of genuine repentance to flow. It
strengthens the faith of the Christian, — even that faith which
works by love and purifies the heart, and works by love.   So
that the true Christian becomes strong in the Lord, and zealous to
do his will, and prepared for every good work. It brightens his
hope of heaven, and greatly increases his spiritual comfort and
joys. Though all worldly comfort should fail, he can rejoice in
God his Saviour, even then. It points to the blessed termination
of his Christian course, — to the joys of immortality, — to the
mansions prepared for him above, — to a seat at God's right hand,
— to a crown and kingdom beyond the skies. All this the word
of God, the aid and influence of the blessed Spirit, can do, and
does accomplish for the Christian. It is a light to his feet and a
lamp to his path, — his guide to truth and duty, to holiness and
peace, to comfort and joy everlasting. It is, then, in the sense
that has been explained, able to prepare him for, and at last to
put him in, the full and blessed possession of the inheritance of
the saints in light.

IMPROVEMENT.

" When a minister of Christ has for several years preached the
gospel to any church and congregation, it is a solemn and affecting duty for him to commend them to God, and to the word of
his grace, and take a final leave of them. To this duty I am now
called. For more than twelve years I have preached, in this
pulpit, to this church and congregation. It becomes me on this
occasion to review my labors, and solemnly inquire how I have
preached to you. Have I followed ' cunningly devised fables,'
the opinions and errors of fallible men, since I undertook to preach
the everlasting gospel to you? Have I withheld from you any
important and essential doctrine of Scripture, endeavoring to explain any one away, by putting false glosses upon, or by giving

7*

wrong interpretations to, any portion of God's word? Certainly I have not knowingly and designedly done this; but have endeavored, in this important part of ministerial duty, to approve myself to God, to my own conscience, and to the conscience of every enlightened hearer. I have not designedly shunned to declare unto you 'all the counsel of God;' to exhibit divine truth to your minds, and impress it upon your hearts, by all the weighty motives suggested by reason and Scripture; to preach to you the unsearchable riches of Christ, — the riches of his wisdom and grace in the plan of salvation through his atoning blood, and the effectual operation of his Spirit. Have I forborne to set the law of God before you, and to prove to you that it is a righteous, holy, and good law? — to bring to your view the nature, extent, and strictness of its requirements, and the awful penalties with which it is sanctioned? Have I ceased to show transgressors their sin and danger, — the dreadful doom that awaits them if they do not repent; and to entreat and beseech them to forsake their sins, repent, believe in Christ, and to be reconciled to God? Have I neglected to warn the decent moralist, the self-righteous pharisee, and the false professor? — to detect their sins, and to expose them to the view of their own consciences, and if possible bring them to repentance? If, in any or all these cases, I have not in some good measure at least discharged the duty of a faithful minister of Christ, you, my hearers, will be swift witnesses against me when we stand together at the bar of Christ. Ah! who of us can stand at that bar, and bear the scrutiny of that solemn and decisive day? Who of us will dare to appear there in his own strength and righteousness, and answer for his unnumbered sins? My hearers, we are all sinners, great sinners. In every duty we have come short. Our best services are stained with sinful imperfections. It would be the highest presumption for us to hope that we shall be acquitted when we stand at Christ's bar, unless our sins have previously been washed away in his atoning blood, and we stand there clothed in the immaculate robe of his righteousness.

I well know, my hearers, that my poor services in the sanctuary have in every respect been defective, — defective in matter and in manner. But what I have most to deplore, and to be humble for before God and before you, is my great want of ardent love to God and the Saviour, and to your immortal souls. Had I felt more strongly the constraining influence of this love, my heart would have glowed with warmer zeal for the glory of God in your salvation. I should have judged more feelingly as the apostle did, ' that if one died for all, then were all dead,' — dead in trespasses and sins, and in imminent danger of eternal death ; I should have had a more lively sense of my great responsibility to God and to you, — of the importance of greater diligence, zeal, and faithfulness in my work, — of the unspeakable worth of your immortal souls, and the imminent danger they are in, if you are still impenitent, of perishing forever. I should have prayed for you with more fervent importunity, preached to you with more zeal and engagedness, and warned you more faithfully and earnestly to flee from the wrath to come, and accept of the mercy offered to you in the gospel. This want of greater love to God and to your souls is, in my apprehension, the greatest sin and imperfection that has attended my public services. Had I always felt more fervent love, I should doubtless have preached and prayed with more zeal and engagedness, and probably with much greater success. I pray God to forgive me this sin ; and I entreat you also to forgive it. And I earnestly beseech him not to suffer any of your souls to perish through my want of love to him and them, and fervor and faithfulness in preaching Christ and him crucified to you.

" But, my hearers, however imperfect and defective my manner of preaching has been, I humbly trust in godly sincerity I have preached to you the plain truths and the all-important doctrines of the gospel ; truths and doctrines which I firmly believe, and by which I wish to live and hope to die. And I have endeavored to state and explain these truths and doctrines in the most plain and intelligible manner. I came not to you, my brethren, ' with excellency of speech or of wisdom.' My aim has always been to use ' great plainness of speech,' that all might understand ; for how otherwise could they be profited by preaching? Learned disquisitions and florid harangues never enlighten and save souls. It has been my conscientious endeavor to feed you with the sincere milk of the word, that you might grow thereby, — in a word to preach Christ and his salvation to you in all the simplicity and plainness of gospel truth.

"And now, my dear hearers, as I must one day stand at the bar of Christ, and answer to him for the truths I have preached to you, and the manner in which I have preached them, must you not also stand at the same bar, and give an account how you have heard and received these truths, and what improvement you have made of them? That will be a solemn day to you and to me. Christ will be our common Judge; and he will judge us both strictly and impartially. That I have preached evangelical truth to you plainly and solemnly, I certainly know. Have you received this truth in faith and love into humble and obedient hearts? And have you brought forth fruit in holy and exemplary lives? Or have you refused to receive and obey divine truth, turned a deaf ear to it, and closed your hearts against it? Let your consciences this day testify. They will testify another day, at the bar of God, if they do not now. This blessed gospel, truly and faithfully preached, will not be in vain. It will bring glory to his *grace* or to his *justice*. It will prove to be the means of your great salvation, or of your greater and more aggravated condemnation. The apostle has assured you that it will be a savor of life unto life, or of death unto death, to the souls of all who hear it. Christ will not come to you by his ministers, and call, invite, and entreat you to be reconciled to God through his blood, and call and invite in vain. If you hear and accept the invitation, your souls will live. Spiritual and eternal life will be begun in you. But if you refuse and reject the kind invitation, your souls will die. They will continue in a state of spiritual death, and at last sink into death eternal. When the minister of Christ thinks of this, how solemn, how momentous, does his work appear! With the apostle he exclaims, ' Who is sufficient for these things?' And you, my hearers, should think of this when you hear the gospel preached, and hear for your lives; remembering that you must give an account how you hear, — remembering that the consequences of hearing, receiving, and obeying the gospel, or of slighting or rejecting its gracious offers, will to you individually be inconceivably important and eternal. I pray God to give you all a hearing ear and an understanding heart, that you may cordially receive and love the truth; that, hearing and obeying the gospel, your souls may live and be nourished up into the words of faith and of good doctrine, to life eternal.

" On this occasion, my Christian brethren and friends I think it proper to give you the following brief account and statement : —

" At the time of my installation, Nov. 29, 1815, this church consisted of forty-eight members. Of these, four have since died, five have been excommunicated, and seventeen dismissed. One has never since been in town, and, whether living or not, I do not know ; another has been absent several years, — though both, if living, still retain their relation to this church; leaving now in town only twenty of the original members.

" Since my installation, one hundred and ninety persons have been received as members of this church, — one hundred and forty-five of them upon their public profession of faith in Christ, — one was restored, and forty-four were received by letters of recommendation from sister churches. Of the whole number, one·hundred and ninety, received since my installation, thirteen have died, four have been excommunicated, and sixty-two regularly dismissed. The whole number of members now in the church is one hundred and thirty-three; twenty of these, however, have removed so far from this town as not to be able to worship with us on the Sabbath, or to attend the communion seasons of the church. During my ministry, fifty-seven adults and one hundred and fifty children have been baptized. During the same time, two hundred and four persons have died in West Bloomfield, being, on an average of the twelve years of my ministry, seventeen each year; twenty of them have died during a little less than eleven months of the present year.

"In reviewing the scenes and events of my twelve years' ministry in this place, I find many things to regret and deplore; and some which ought to excite my warmest gratitude and yours, and call forth our united praise and thanksgiving to God. I have great reason to regret the deficiencies and imperfections which have attended my public services; and my want of more zeal, fervor, and faithfulness in discharging the various and important duties of the pastoral and ministerial office; and that so little success has attended my labors. For my own sinful deficiencies I ought to be humbled, and I desire to be humbled, before God and before you.

"I see reason, also, to deplore some events which have taken place in this society; in particular and especially the introduction and prevalence of an unscriptural opinion and dangerous error respecting a most important point of doctrine, — the real divinity of our Lord Jesus Christ. This opinion supposes him to be an inferior, subordinate, and dependent God, deprives him of his real divinity, and degrades him to the rank of a creature. It, of course, destroys his atonement, and leaves the perishing sinner without help or hope. By the introduction and prevalence of this heresy, and by the death or removal of a number of able members of the church and congregation, the ability of the society to support the gospel is materially diminished. If, however, they will be united and engaged in this important enterprise, there is still ability in the society to provide a competent support for a minister of Christ, without feeling it to be a burden. And it is my earnest desire and prayer, my Christian friends, that you will unitedly engage in this highly important concern.

"During my ministry, God has not wholly withheld from us the blessed influences of his Spirit. At two seasons, especially, the Spirit descended upon us like rain, and converts sprang up, as willows by the water-courses. This — the greatest of all blessings — should awaken and excite our warmest gratitude and praise to God. I see in this congregation some of the spiritual children which God graciously gave me as the fruits of my ministry; and they will ever be dear to my heart.

" During my labors in this place, I and my family have received from you, my brethren and friends, many tokens of friendship, and deeds of kindness and liberality ; for all which we return you our united and cordial thanks. What is done to the least of Christ's servants, out of love to him, he considers as done to himself, and will not fail to reward it. May he reward you, for all your kindness and liberality to us, a thousand fold.

" And now, dear brethren and friends, I must take my leave of you. And I do earnestly and fervently commend you to God, to his care, protection, and blessing, and to the word of his grace, which is able to build you up in the holy faith and practice of the gospel, and at last give you an inheritance incorruptible and undefiled, among all his redeemed and sanctified children, in his eternal, heavenly kingdom. Amen."

After his dismission, Dr. Fitch continued to preach occasionally till within a short time of his decease. In the summer of 1828, then in the seventy-second year of his age, in company with his wife, he visited New England. He called at Williamstown; then proceeded as far east as Boston; and took Canterbury, Norwich, and New Haven in his way, on his return home. It was his last visit to the scenes of his childhood and principal labors, and was a source of much satisfaction to him during the remainder of his days.*

* The following letter, from his Honor Lieut. Governor Childs, is inserted with pleasure, and will be read with interest: —

"Boston, Feb. 11, 1843.

" *Rev. and Dear Sir :* — It gave me great pleasure to learn that you had prepared for publication a sketch of the life and character of the good Dr. Fitch, — the venerable instructor of my youth. It gave me a melancholy pleasure to meet him, in the fall of 1828, at that advanced period of life

Abating the ordinary infirmities of age, and an injury of his foot, received in 1824, by which he was lamed, he continued to enjoy a good degree of health and activity of body, for a man of his years, until within a few months of his death. He had been, at times, troubled with an asthmatic affection, but was able to ride and walk out. His breathing was at times laborious, and, when reclining, was painfully so. When sitting or walking, he was comfortable. His appetite for food was good; and he continued to enjoy the society of his friends as much as ever. At times he expressed doubts as to his continuing long in life; still he evidently did not anticipate a sudden departure from this world.

when of necessity the powers of body and mind were gradually failing. He seemed, however, cheerful and pleasant, and was very happy in meeting some of his former pupils and friends. He evidently felt that he had nearly finished his course on earth. He exhibited, however, a calm resignation to the will of his heavenly Father, and expressed a confident hope of a glorious immortality. This strong hope gave unusual brightness to a face naturally beaming with kindness and benignity. I well recollect the deep impression, which his visit left upon my mind, that I should see his face no more. It was his last visit to Berkshire. His friends were all happy to see him again, and he apparently received much comfort and joy in their society. Much of his conversation related to occurrences of by-gone days, the mention of which interested and animated him much. As a token of the respect which we entertained for our venerable President, a few friends in Pittsfield presented him with some mementos of their esteem, which he kindly and gratefully received, and which consisted of a suit of clothes, and something over a hundred dollars in money. Permit me again to express my high gratification that you have prepared for the press a work which will perpetuate the memory of a great and good man. Please accept my kindest regards.

"With much respect, yours truly,   H. H. CHILDS."

Hence he arranged nothing as to his family or effects. During all this time his mind was tranquil, and evidently much upon those things which are unseen and eternal. His confidence in the wisdom and rectitude of God's dispensations appeared to be strong and consoling. In this state of health and happy frame of mind he continued until Thursday, March 21st, 1833. On the morning of that day no material alteration was discovered. He appeared much as usual. At noon he took some light refreshment in his room, instead of dining with the family as he had usually done. After dinner, on the return of his wife, he observed that he should like to lie down, as he felt that he could get some rest. With a very little assistance he walked to the bed, and laid himself down. As Mrs. Fitch was drawing the clothes about his feet, she cast her eyes upon him, and perceived that he had risen upon his elbows, and was struggling for breath. She exclaimed, " You breathe very hard." Receiving no answer, she hastened to summon the family together,— in time only to see him gasp two or three times, and all was over. Thus suddenly closed a long and useful life.

" It is blessed to go when so ready to die."

He died about the same age of his father, — nearly seventy-seven — without a groan; or rather fell asleep, serenely closing his eyes upon this world of sin and vanity, where there is little more than the joys of union and the tears of separation.

8

" At *noon-day* came the cry, —
   ' To meet thy God prepare;'
He heard, and caught his Captain's eye, —
   Then strong in faith and prayer,

" His spirit, with a bound,
   Left its encumbering clay;
His tent at sunset on the ground
   A darkened ruin lay.

" The pains of death are past,
   Labor and sorrow cease;
And, life's long warfare closed at last,
   His soul is found in peace."

The next Lord's day his remains were conveyed
to the church, where he had so often and so faithfully held forth the word of life; and where an impressive and appropriate discourse was delivered to
a crowded assembly, by the Rev. Julius Steele.
The sermon was not published. From the manuscript copy in our possession, we make the following extract. It was founded on Romans viii. 28:
*And we know that all things work together for good
to them that love God.* " Dr. Fitch was a man of
solid science and varied literature. He was a man
of great native mildness and amiableness of disposition. As a scholar, he ranked with the first of his
age in this country. As a companion, he was easy,
affable, and winning. As a teacher of youth, the
hundreds in our land to whom he imparted instruction are his memorial; and through whom, ' he being dead, yet speaketh.' As a Christian, he was pro-
verbially meek and humble. As a minister, he

seemed ever mindful of the apostolic injunction, 'not to think of himself more highly than he ought to think.' His error, if error it can be called, consisted in his undervaluing himself as a minister of Christ. His praise is in all the churches around us, and rose as his sun of life declined. As a co-presbyter, we loved him as a brother, and venerated him as a father. We all loved Father Fitch."

" As a writer, Dr. Fitch ranked high. He was classical and perspicuous. As a reasoner, he was consecutive, pertinent, and accurate. Possessed of fine and tender feelings himself, he seemed ever most unwilling to utter that which would unnecessarily wound the feelings of his hearers. He was eminently a son of consolation. Those most edified by his preaching were the more intelligent and cultivated part of the community. His manner of life previous to his becoming a settled pastor inclined him to aim more at benefiting his hearers through the understanding than to influence and affect them by addressing the passions. He was no blustering declaimer. In plainness and gospel simplicity, he reasoned concerning 'righteousness, temperance, and judgment to come.' He dwelt much upon ' Christ and him crucified,' — upon the marvellous love of God to man in *that unspeakable gift.* And as he taught so he practised. He exemplified the benevolence of the gospel in a high degree.

" It may be expected that I should speak of him as the husband of one wife, and the father of a

family. Incompetent as I feel myself to be to delineate any part of the life and character of this
good man, I am entirely incapable of doing anything like justice when I come to speak of him in
the private walks of life. ' A kinder husband,' said
his bereaved and mourning consort, as we stood
bending over the cold remains of departed worth, ' a
kinder husband the world never furnished, woman
never had.' The nearest and dearest relations of life
he sustained, I had almost said, without a fault. In
all his domestic relations he seemed to be *blameless.*
Happy are they above most, who can call such a
man either husband or father. Few had more
friends, and more deservedly. Confidence he never
betrayed. With the feelings or reputation of a
neighbor he never trifled. To the best his house
could furnish, those who called upon him always
received a hearty welcome. Many are his debtors.
He lived to do good. He lived on the promised reward of the saints at the resurrection of the just.
The good man's labors are now ended. His trials
are now over. He now sleeps in death. Last
Thursday, not at midnight, but at mid-day, the cry
was heard, ' Behold, the bridegroom cometh.' Our
departed friend hastened and delayed not to obey the
call. He was all ready to obey so hasty a sum-
mons. He arose from his seat, retired to his
sleeping-room, laid himself down, and as soon as
words can relate, slept in death's cold embrace, not
to awake again ' till the heavens be no more.'

Mourning friends, the good, the great, the amiable man, the valued neighbor, the tried and faithful friend, the fond husband, endeared by a thousand kind offices, the affectionate and tender father, the learned, pious, and estimable minister, is no more on earth. From all the fond and long-cherished endearments below, death has suddenly and forever removed him. Of all earthly scenes he has taken a last, a long farewell, and gone up to that rest which 'remaineth to the people of God.' "

On a monument erected over his grave was the following inscription : " In memory of the Rev. Ebenezer Fitch, D. D., who was born in Canterbury, Ct., 1756; graduated at Yale College, 1777; tutor in the same about 8 years; President of Williams College 22 years; Pastor of the Church in West Bloomfield 12 years. He died March 21, 1833, aged 76 years. The righteous shall be in everlasting remembrance."

Mrs. Fitch died in the family of her daughter, Mrs. Folsom, at Cleveland, O., Nov. 21, 1834. Her death was peaceful and triumphant. She lived and died in the faith and hope of the gospel.

5*

CHAPTER VII.

HILE President Fitch was in Europe, he traced the origin and history of his ancestors back through many generations; besides, he always kept an exact account of all the branches of his family settled in this country. After his decease, all his manuscripts fell into the hands of his son, the Rev. C. Fitch, whose house with its contents was soon after con- sumed by fire. His cotemporaries, like himself, have nearly all passed away in the lapse of eighty-six years; so that very general incidents of his life only

(90)

can now be recovered from oblivion. This statement is made with a view to anticipate and obviate
an objection to which this sketch of the life of Dr.
Fitch is liable, from its deficiency in minute information, and in a discriminating estimate of his character. And in this connection it may with propriety
be stated that he rarely published any of the productions of his pen. A historical sketch of Col.
Ephraim Williams and of Williams College, published in the Mass. Historical Collections, in 1802;
a Baccalaureate Discourse in 1799; a funeral discourse in 1812; and a missionary sermon at Hudson, N. Y., in 1814, include all his publications of
which we have any knowledge. From a few scattered and necessarily imperfect sources must now be
obtained all our information respecting this truly excellent man.

After the brief general survey which has now been
taken of the more prominent events of his life, we
would attempt, as a service due to his memory and
friends, to add something more respecting his manner of life, and his qualifications for those important
spheres in which he was called to move. Instead of
a full-drawn portrait of his character, however, we
are able to present only an imperfect outline.

Our readers will be able to form some general
estimate of Dr. Fitch's character from what is contained in the following letters, which we here introduce with much pleasure.

The first is from the Rev. President Day, of Yale

College. — " My particular acquaintance with President Fitch was of short continuance, while I was a
tutor in Williams College in the years 1797 and 1798.
The institution had then been in operation but a few
years, yet it was rapidly advancing, under the active
and successful superintendence of Dr. Fitch. At that
early period there were not very frequent calls for stern
and vigorous discipline. The President was vigilant
and faithful, and enjoyed the confidence and cordial
co-operation of the subordinate instructors. He was
endeared to the students by his affectionate regard
for their best interests, and his self-denying labors
for their welfare. In the common intercourse of society, he was social, instructive and benevolent. He
was unwearied in his endeavors to promote the welfare of those within the reach of his influence. I
considered him a man of sincere and stable piety.
I rarely heard him preach. His discourses, so far as
I had the means of knowing, were sound, practical
compositions, without an affectation of profound research, or refined metaphysical speculation. He
appeared to aim to be practically useful, rather than
to make a display of profound and original powers
of investigation. In the endearments of domestic
life he was distinguished for affectionate kindness,
and assiduous attention to the wants and wishes of
his family."

The next is from James W. Robbins, Esq., who
was graduated at Williams College in 1802. — " I
spent near seven years in Williamstown while Dr.

Fitch was president, and a part of the time boarded in his family. During more than thirty years, which have since elapsed, the acquaintance which I have had an opportunity to form with other men, has not lessened the estimate which I then entertained of his character. Perhaps the most prominent qualities of his heart and disposition were purity and benevolence. As a natural consequence of the purity of his own intentions, he was very seldom suspicious of others; and his benevolent feelings were awakened whenever an object was presented adapted to their excitement; and his benevolence, when carried out in acts of kindness and charity, was limited only by the extent of his ability. As a scholar, his literary acquirements were highly respectable. His official duties in connection with college, and the many cares necessarily incident to the management of a numerous and dependent family, did not leave him sufficient leisure for extensive scientific investigations, or for becoming acquainted with the whole circle of general literature. As a teacher, he was faithful and communicative; and those students who were instructed by him during their senior year, will never forget the ability and interest with which he explained and illustrated the writings of Locke, Paley, and Vattel. As a Christian, he was sincere and devout; desirous of knowing his duty, and, when ascertained, was ready, beyond most men, to perform it. As a preacher, he was more instructive than impressive, but none could faithfully listen to his ser-

mons without improvement. Dr. Fitch labored
assiduously for the interest of the college over which
he was called to preside, and for the moral and intellectual improvement of the young men who resorted
to that institution."

" I shall never forget," writes the Rev. John Nelson, of Leicester, who was graduated at Williams
College in 1807, " the first interview which I had
with the venerable President Fitch. I entered college young and inexperienced, and with an over-
powering dread of so high a dignitary as I then supposed the president of a college must be. It was
with a trembling step that I entered the study of Dr.
Fitch with my credentials in hand; but there was
something so kind, so cordial, so fatherly in his greet-
ings, that my heart went forth to him at once as to
a guardian friend in whom I could safely trust. Nor
did I ever find anything in the spirit, the conduct, or
the bearing of my venerated President, which weak-
ened, or in any way effaced those early impressions.
On the contrary, while he faithfully maintained the
discipline of college, I ever found him ready to extend to all both the care and kindness of an affectionate guardian and friend. But I did not fully
appreciate the domestic, the social, and the Christian,
as well as the official excellences of Dr. Fitch, till
at a subsequent period I became more intimately
associated with him as a member of the college faculty, and a boarder in his family. During the two
years in which I sustained these relations to him, I

was more and more impressed with the rare virtues
and excellences which composed his character. His
attachment and kindness to his numerous family I
found to be almost unexampled. His benevolence
to the poor and suffering flowed forth in one continued stream. His hospitality seemed to be unbounded
Christian hospitality. His intercourse with his friends
was free, cheerful, and yet characterized by an all-
pervading spirit of piety. As the head of a college,
Dr. Fitch was diligent, faithful and efficient. As an
instructor, he was clear, safe, and, to a good degree,
able. As a preacher, he was profitable and interesting, and sometimes powerful. As a Christian, he
caused his light to shine brightly and uniformly.
Had he been less modest, less retiring, less at home,
his reputation, no doubt, would have stood much
higher. Had he gone abroad, and appeared before
the public like many other distinguished men of his
time, his name would have had a high place among
theirs."

" Concerning President Fitch," the venerable Dr.
John Woodbridge writes: " I have only to say he
was truly an estimable man, and was a great bene-
factor to the college in the early period of its history. He was an excellent scholar in the various departments of classical learning. To those who desired it, he taught Hebrew and French, as I was
told, with a good degree of thoroughness; and he
appeared ever desirous of doing all in his power to
promote the respectability and usefulness of his pu-

pils. His paternal eye was on them while in college, and followed them, I cannot doubt, with lively solicitude, after they had been withdrawn from his special care into the various walks of public life. I knew him only as the presiding officer and teacher; but I could bear witness to the kindness of his heart when I was in trouble and needed his sympathy and advice. For his counsel and encouragement, given in my early years, I owe him a debt of gratitude. In my review of early days, Dr. Fitch is one of those individuals whose character brightens by the reflections of the past. He had a mild, dark eye, and a countenance beaming with goodness. In the various relations of life he was, I am sure, a pattern of kindness and fidelity. His orthodoxy was straight-forward and explicit, like his own honest and noble soul. If he had any fault as a teacher and disciplinarian, it was the excess of lenity, more than needless severity. He was, perhaps, sometimes too irresolute and wavering for the full maintenance of his authority. His menace might have been sometimes more terrible than the execution. He might in some cases have entreated when a command was necessary. He might occasionally have wept, when he ought to have inflicted punishment. This, at least, was said by some *not very friendly to his administration.* The location of the college at that time, and the peculiar circumstances of the country, placed him under circumstances of disadvantage and discouragement. These disadvantages do not now exist. Yet he did a great work for learning and religion in his day, and helped to lay broad and deep foundations for coming ages. Peace to his memory; and may the blessing of God descend upon the institution he loved, in answer to his many prayers.

" The information I can give concerning him can be of little consequence in his biography. I remember him as if I had seen him yesterday; and yet I cannot paint the impression he made upon my youthful mind."

In his excellent address before the Society of Alumni, in 1862, the Hon. A. C. Paige drops the passing remark: " Our respected President (Dr. Fitch), whose learning was only equalled by his spotless virtue, and who was as conspicuous for his piety as for his guileless simplicity, has long since been lifted up among the sons of light."

> " Peace to the just man's memory, — let it grow
> Greener with years, and blossom through the flight
> Of ages; let the mimic canvas show
> His calm, benevolent features; let the light
> Stream on his deeds of love, that shunned the sight
> Of all but heaven, and, in the book of fame,
> The glorious record of his virtues write,
> And hold it up to men, and bid them claim
> A palm like his, and catch from him the hallowed flame."

In the following general summary respecting Dr. Fitch, we shall aim to keep in mind the venerable maxim, " *De mortuis nil, nisi bonum ;*" and at the same time not to give any overdrawn statement of his good qualities.

In personal appearance, Dr. Fitch was rather below than above the middling stature. " His countenance was grave, but rather pleasant than austere. His appearance and deportment were always gentlemanly and dignified; though sometimes, through his great modesty, not marked with perfect ease and elegance." His personal appearance was certainly much in his favor.

" While I was a member of Williams College," writes the poet Bryant, " Dr. Fitch was President, and instructor of the senior class. I have a vivid recollection of his personal appearance, — a square-built man, of dark complexion, and black, arched eyebrows. To me his manner was kind and courteous, and I remember it with pleasure." He was a man of good presence and comeliness; combining dignity with cheerfulness.

" Dr. Fitch," says Professor Dewey, " was a man of fine personal appearance, of rather courtly manners, and dignified carriage."

As a Christian, Dr Fitch was sincere, devout, consistent, and uniform. He aimed to keep his heart with all diligence, and adorn the doctrine of God his Saviour in all things. It is the united testimony of those who knew him best, that he was remarkably exemplary as a Christian. No one could be long in his society, says a competent judge, without perceiving that his mind was strongly imbued with religious feeling. He was evidently a Christian of a high order. He was not without a share of those failings which are common to fallen man.

"But e'en his failings leaned to virtue's side."

" In my early years," writes Mrs. S., " I was deeply impressed with the consistency and perfection of his Christian character; ever displaying, as he did, the most entire and childlike submission to the will of his heavenly Father. Indeed, whenever I have endeavored to conceive of a person fully under the influence, and moulded by the pure and ennobling principles of the gospel, my mind involuntarily recurs to Father Fitch as affording a lovely exemplification."

Dr. Fitch possessed *native powers of mind* of a high, if not of a preëminent order. They were characterized by solid strength, rather than brilliancy. They were capable of deliberate and manly, rather than high-wrought efforts. His memory was strong and retentive ; hence the large fund of useful anecdote which was ever at his command, and which he employed with happy success at the recitations of his pupils, and to enliven and instruct in the social circle. His patient industry in the pursuit of knowledge, added to his original capacity for acquiring it, gave him a high standing among his classmates in college, and a high place among his literary associates in subsequent years. During his presidency at Williamstown he was somewhat extensively known as a man of solid and varied learning. " He was a man," says Professor Dewey, " of strong powers of mind. The more difficult parts of the philosophy of his day, natural and moral, so far as the means of investigation were at his command, he readily comprehended and made his own; and that knowledge he could easily transfer into the minds of others. I well remember many points which he presented and illustrated to our class in an indelible manner. Had chemistry been taught in his education, he would have made a chemist of high respectability." Dr. Fitch was a man of a well-balanced mind. It may be said of him as Chalmers said of Urquhart: " He had the amplitude of genius, but none of its irregularities. There was no shooting forth of mind in one direction so as to give a prominency to certain acquisitions. He was neither a mere geometer, nor a mere linguist, nor a mere metaphysician; he was all put together; alike distinguished by the fulness and harmony of his powers." The cast of his mind was practical, rather than brilliant.

In his younger days he wrote some poetry very creditable to his taste and genius. A niece once requested him to furnish her with some lines for a mourning piece, which she was embroidering in memory of a departed sister. He wrote the following impromptu : —

" When thy dear Saviour wakes the dead,
    And bids thy dust arise,
  Then thou shalt leave this humble bed,
    And meet him in the skies."

Among his papers that were destroyed, his children well recollect there was a manuscript book containing a large number (probably all) of his poetic articles. A few of his pieces have come into our hands. We have concluded to insert the two following productions of his youthful pen : —

" ODE TO INNOCENCE.

" Fairest daughter of the skies,
    Stranger to the least offence,
  Nobly scorning all disguise,
    Lovely, smiling Innocence.

" Deck'd in robes of purest snow,
    Bright and fair as summer's morn,
  Beauteous as the flowers that blow,
    Meads and valleys to adorn.

" Not the myrtle's cooling shade,
    Not the rural lover's bower,
  Not the calm, sequestered glade,
    Blooming with each fragrant flower ;

" Not the bliss that Science pours
    O'er the bright, enraptured mind,
  When on eagle wings she soars
    To the utmost bounds assigned ;

" Not the honors of the great,
    Titles of a sounding name,
  Splendor, power, and pomp of state,
    Towers and sceptres, wealth and **fame,** —
9*

" Can to bliss he knew before,
    When in thy pure garb arrayed,
His pained bosom e'er restore,
    Who from thee has hapless strayed.

" Choicest friend of mortals here,
    None, without thee, can be blest ;
Yet thou loveliest dost appear
    In the blooming fair one's breast.

" There, in charms that ever please,
    We thy loveliness behold ;
Such, 'mid Eden's bowery trees,
    Adam saw in Eve of old.

" Such in fair Honora's mind,
    Bright as morning's pearly dew,
With each gentle virtue joined,
    We with pleasing rapture view.

" May she, O celestial fair !
    From thy footsteps never rove ;
But thy purest pleasure share,
    Till she join the train above."

The affecting circumstance which gave rise to the following lines was this : A young lady, an acquaintance of his, commenced life with an ample fortune, and most flattering prospects of usefulness and happiness, but in one year to a day from her marriage lay a corpse. They were written when he was a youth.

"BREVITY OF LIFE.

"Ah ! Delia, art thou then no more ?
    Is this thine early doom ?

Are all life's flattering prospects o'er,
   And thou beneath the tomb?

" Is this the end of hopes so bright,
   Fair hopes of happy days,
Of years, long years, of pure delight? —
   So dies the meteor's blaze!

" Pale are those cheeks which late were warm
   And fresh as blooming May,
Alas! too soon that lovely form
   Has found a bed of clay!

" Ah! hapless youth, she's gone, she's dead;
   All faded are her charms.
Delia, thy lovely Delia's fled
   Forever from thy arms.

" Lo, in her clay-cold bed she lies,
   Beneath the verdant sod,
While her departed spirit flies
   To meet her Saviour God.

" Oft to her grave, at close of day,
   Wilt thou, sad swain, repair,
Weep o'er her dear departed clay,
   And mourn thy Delia there.

" Oft, tender maids, at spring's return,
   With gentle swains shall come,
And, while her early fate they mourn,
   Strew flowers o'er her tomb.

" But thou, alas! afflicted youth,
   What comfort canst thou find? —
She was all gentleness and truth,
   Meek, tender, fair and kind.

" She thy fond hopes and wishes crowned ;
    Thy joys were bright and pure ;
To thee all nature smil'd around ;
    Thy bliss appeared secure.

" Ah, sad reverse!   But, oh, forbear
    To murmur or complain !
Shall man, rash man, presumptuous dare
    Heaven's counsels to arraign ?

" From His kind hand the blessing came, —
    The choicest Delia proved ;
. What once he gave, may he not claim,
    And still be feared and loved ?

" One pledge of chaste connubial love
    She's left to soothe thy woe ;
Let this a father's kindness prove,
    His care and culture know.

" Let this sweet babe some balm impart,
    To dry a sister's tears,
Heal a fond mother's bleeding heart,
    And bless thy future years.

" Learn hence, fond youth, how false and vain
    Earth's noblest pleasures prove ;
Her brightest joys are dashed with pain ;
    True bliss is found above ! "

Dr. Fitch engaged with ardor and perseverance in
the investigation of every subject to which he turned
his attention.   Still, his scholarship seems to have
been general, rather than confined to any particular
branch of science.   He understood thoroughly the
whole course of study pursued in our colleges at

that period. With the Latin and Greek languages he was very familiar. The Hebrew, too, received a share of his attention, to which he and his cotemporaries were, no doubt, encouraged by that distinguished Hebrician, President Stiles. He was likewise familiar with the French language. His handwriting was very fair and rather superior, — better when he was seventy than when a tutor in college.

Dr. Fitch was well qualified, in most respects, to have the *instruction and guardianship* of young men. It would not, probably, be considered strictly correct to assert that he was, on the whole, preëminently qualified to stand at the head of a college. He possessed the talent of government, however, to that degree that he was revered and beloved by his numerous pupils. Some have thought that he was deficient in decision or firmness. His tenderness of feeling may have led him, in some instances, to shrink from enforcing or executing all that he had threatened in case of delinquency or disorder. Still he was not strikingly deficient in this trait of character. The instances were not common in which he fell short, in the issue, of doing all that wholesome discipline required. "For years," says one of his associates in office, "we had no case in which Dr. Fitch did not bear up his end well in the government of college." The same valued friend and former instructor adds: "Dr. Fitch was too good a man, too pure in his feelings, too affectionate toward his pupils, too desirous of the happiness of

all around him, to allow me to take up any little
failure in some trait of character." The *friends* of
Dr. Fitch would be the last to deny that in connection with his many excellences he had a share of
those imperfections which belong to man. But to
dwell upon these would be productive of no good.
If any one should wish to see his failings delineated,
it must be done by some other pen than ours.

The president of a college is regarded as a kind
of parent or guardian to all the young men. And
he must give attention to all their inquiries and
wants, whether real or imaginary. Dr. Fitch, from
his early education, natural kindness, practical wisdom and experience in teaching, was peculiarly fitted
to meet these demands upon his time and patience.
He almost invariably secured the entire confidence
and respect of his pupils. He showed himself to be
their friend; and they in turn cheerfully reciprocated
his friendship. He treated them as young gentlemen, and they rarely failed to be gentlemanly in
return. " The instructor was forgotten in the friend
and father." We have almost invariably heard those
who were graduated at Williams College during his
presidency, speak of him in the highest terms of respect and veneration. And why should it not be so?
For, not only over their studies, but their health,
their morals, their present and eternal welfare, he
watched with paternal care and anxious solicitude.
As a consequence, few instructors have been more
uniformly and gratefully remembered by their pupils.

As a preacher, Dr. Fitch's qualities partook of the solid rather than of the brilliant and showy. His sermons, so far as we have had the means of ascertaining, were characterized by plainness of style, clearness of illustration, soundness of argument, and the simplicity of the gospel. His manner was solemn, earnest, and affectionate. He was a biblical, instructive, and practical preacher. In his religious sentiments he was strictly orthodox. He belonged to the school of Edwards. A clergyman of reputation says of him: " His accuracy in language and rhetorical correctness in composition were perhaps carried to excess. His delivery was good. His voice was full and sonorous, and his enunciation distinct and forcible. In composition he evidently inclined to the pathetic."

From his Baccalaureate discourse, delivered in 1799, from the text, — *But covet earnestly the best gifts ; and yet show I unto you a more excellent way*, — we make the following brief extract: —

" However desirable and worthy of pursuit the best natural and acquired gifts may be, there is still a more excellent and glorious way. This is the way of holiness; which leads directly and certainly to present peace and future happiness. Talents without piety, gifts without grace, will not profit you at last. Splendid abilities may dazzle the eyes of men, and command their admiration and applause; but true virtue alone can procure the divine favor, and ensure the rewards of a better life. This alone gives real worth and importance to genius and erudition, to brilliant talents and extensive knowledge. What do wit, genius, and learning now avail Hume and Bolingbroke, Shaftsbury and Voltaire? Prostituted as these talents were by them to the infamous cause of infidelity and vice, what purpose do they now answer, but as flaming torches to light them to the lowest pits of their infernal prison, and show them, in tenfold horrors, the regions of eternal darkness? What would they now give for one cheering ray of that heavenly religion which they once hooted and despised, — for one drop of his atoning blood, whom, with the rage and malice of fiends, they so often reviled and blasphemed? You, my young friends, have formed, I trust, a more just estimate of the worth of religion. But its real value cannot, in the present state, be fully told or conceived. When the splendors of eternal day shall burst upon your astonished vision, or the pit of endless despair yawn upon you, then, and not till then, will you know its infinite worth, — its high and everlasting importance."

But the crowning excellence of Dr. Fitch as a preacher, remains to be mentioned. He was wise to win souls to Christ. During his residence at Williamstown, numbers were hopefully converted through his instrumentality, and prepared for extensive usefulness in Zion. And during his twelve years' ministry in West Bloomfield, though his congregation was not large, and he in the evening of his days, still the admission to that church averaged *sixteen* annually. Not a year passed, while he ministered to that people, but that some were brought out of darkness into marvellous light, and confessed Christ before men.

It hardly need be added that Dr. Fitch took a deep and lively interest in the cause of *education in general*. Could he devote eight years of his early

life to the duties of an instructor in Yale College,
three years to the office of preceptor at Williamstown, and twenty-two to the presidency of the college ; educate some young men almost entirely at
his own expense ; take an early and prominent part
in the efforts of the American Education Society,
and in the establishment of the Theological Seminary at Auburn, — unless the cause of education,
especially the preparation of pious young men for
the gospel ministry, was with him an object of ab-
sorbing interest?

Dr. Fitch was truly *a lover of good men.* He was
given to hospitality. He was liberal to all who
called upon him, as much so as his means would
allow. He was the best beloved by those who knew
him best. He made many friends, and had no enemies. It may be questioned whether he had an
enemy in the world. Perhaps no man was ever
more beloved by all his neighbors wherever he lived.
His doors were freely opened, and all his guests were
made to feel that they were welcome to the best
that his house could furnish. He never amassed
much wealth; he had little more than a bare com-
petency. Still, by joining economy with liberality,
he passed his days in circumstances of comfort,
honor, and content. His virtues and learning were
his richest inheritance. His best hopes were his
treasures laid up in heaven.

During his presidency, he aided some young men
in obtaining an education probably beyond his pecu-
10

niary ability. One of them, the day after his grad-
uation, on taking leave of the President, assured him,
if ever he should become able to do so, he would
remunerate him for his kindness and confidence.
More than twenty years afterward, when Dr. Fitch
had retired from the ministry and was receiving no
regular income, he had contracted some debts which
he had not the means of paying, besides living in a
house which he did not own. All unexpectedly there
arrived at his dwelling in West Bloomfield, one
evening, an individual whom Dr. Fitch did not rec-
ognize. It was soon, however, ascertained to be
Gordon H. Backus, a nephew of Mrs. Fitch, and
who was graduated at Williams College in 1806.
He had been successful in his profession as a lawyer
in Richmond, Va., and had now come to redeem the
pledge, given years before, that, if ever he should be
able to do so, he would give his venerable friend and
patron something better than thanks for his education. He ascertained that evening Dr. Fitch's pecuniary circumstances. The next day he presented
Dr. Fitch with a receipt for all his debts, a deed of
the house in which he lived, and two thousand dollars in cash. " Cast thy bread upon the waters; for
thou shalt find it after many days."

Dr. Fitch was a man of *untiring industry.* If he
was not, strictly speaking, a diligent and laborious
student; if he was not uniformly and indefatigably
engaged in the pursuit of some great and worthy
object; if he was not always employed about that

which pertained to his office or profession, still he was a remarkably industrious man. None of his time was suffered to run to waste. Every hour of his life appeared to be conscientiously devoted to some valuable purpose. With him no hours could strictly be called leisure hours. Besides the needful time for repose and refreshment, he was uniformly occupied in his study, in his official duties, in his garden or wood-house, in attending to his domestic concerns, or in some way promoting the good of his fellow-men. His labors were always arduous, and sometimes excessive. Besides performing all his domestic and collegiate duties, he frequently preached on the Sabbath, and sometimes for months in succession; and the calls on him for services abroad were somewhat numerous. Under the pressure of so many cares and labors, his constitution, not originally remarkably firm, must have failed but for his regular exercise in the open air, to which he habitually accustomed himself. There is much salutary counsel and practical wisdom in the following sentence contained in a letter to his son, then just settled in the ministry. " The garden has been *my* physician, — let it be *yours.*" During the twenty-two years of his presidency at Williamstown, the regular performance of his official duties was never known to be interrupted by sickness, but once, for a single week. His constitution was preserved, to a great extent, hale and vigorous till near the close of life.

The source of Dr. Fitch's *support and comfort in*

the day of affliction and trial may be inferred from
the following letter, which is strikingly characteristic
of him. It was written near the close of his life,
and addressed to two of his children, then deeply
afflicted. " About noon to-day, I took from the office
your letter, conveying to us the distressing tidings
of your dear little Harriet's death. This is indeed
an afflictive dispensation ; but no doubt perfectly
wise and good. My thoughts have repeatedly anticipated it, and I may almost say foreboded it. Such
precious gifts as your two lovely babes appeared
almost too much for any imperfect mortals to receive
and safely retain. So prone are the hearts of God's
partially sanctified children to doat on such rich gifts
from his munificent hand, and even to idolize them,
that he often sees it to be best and necessary for
their good, soon to take them back. This he unquestionably has a right to do, and always will do,
when he sees it will promote the spiritual good of
those he loves. What son or daughter is there
whom the father does not chasten for their profit and
growth in grace ? This he does, sometimes more
and sometimes less severely, and always in covenant
love and faithfulness to his children. Watts says : —

> ' The brightest things below the sky
>   Give but a flattering light;
> We should suspect some danger nigh,
>   Where we possess delight.'

Sad experience often teaches the Christian that this

sentiment is true. When our hearts are too much set on any earthly object, there is always reason to apprehend that our heavenly Father will, in kindness, take that object from us. And shall we complain of an act of kindness and tenderness in *him* whose love to his children is unfailing? This love always directs Him to consult their highest and best interest in all his dealings; some of which, to answer this kind and benevolent purpose, must be trying and afflictive. Prosperity is much more dangerous to them than adversity; worldly comforts, than disappointments and afflictions. I do not say, my dear children, that your affections were in an uncommon degree set upon your lovely babes. But it would be very natural if they were. The temptation was unusually strong, and you must have had more than a common share of grace to resist and overcome it. Perhaps you find they were, and now see the reason why your kind heavenly Father has thus dealt with you. If so, this should be a motive to the most humble submission to the divine will, and entire resignation to this afflicting providence. It is a severe trial of your faith, patience, and acquiescence in the pleasure of Him who does all things well. His grace can, and I trust will, not only support you, but comfort you under this sore bereavement, and bring you out of this furnace of affliction, as gold purified by fire. We deeply feel the affliction ourselves, and tenderly sympathize with you. It is our earnest prayer that God will be pleased to spare your little

son, and not add sorrow to sorrow. But he knows
what is best. His pleasure will be done, and it is
our duty to acquiesce, whatever it may be."

In bringing this biographical sketch of President
Fitch to a close, we are deeply and painfully sensible
of its imperfections. While preparing it, we have
often been led to wonder that one so useful, distinguished, and deserving has been hitherto overlooked,
while many inferior to him have been largely noticed.
The preceding representations of him, we are fully
satisfied, fall below what they ought to have been.
We have not reached the standard at which we
aimed. But our consolation is that we have done
what we could to rescue from oblivion the life and
character of one who deserves a far better and more
extended memorial. Though Dr. Fitch was modest
and unobtrusive, and never appeared to be reaching
after applause or popularity, still, the life which he
lived, the character which he sustained, and the
labors he performed, ought to secure for him a precious and enduring record in the history of his times.
And now, with the addition of a single paragraph,
we lay down our pen.

As a companion, father, and friend, Dr. Fitch was
all that his nearest connections could desire him to
be. "A kinder husband," said his bereaved widow,
"the world never furnished. His unremitting attention to me, during my late illness, contributed greatly
to his being taken so suddenly to the grave." Another member of his family remarks : " I think I can

unhesitatingly say that I never knew one better calculated to render a home-circle cheerful and happy
than my deceased father. Anticipating every wish
of wife and children, and in his own manners uniformly bland and affectionate, the cheerful and
happy influence of his presence and conversation
was daily felt throughout our whole circle. He
was also characterized by a remarkable equanimity
of temper. In the varied trials incident to every
family's experience, during my whole life I never
saw his bright, sun-lit countenance shaded by a
frown; nor did I ever have any evidence that his
equilibrium of mind was disturbed." As a *father*,
he was uniformly affectionate, kind and provident.
His children invariably revered, loved, and obeyed
him, and were emulous to please him. As a *friend*,
few have been more highly esteemed and valued.
" I know not," says Dr. Davis, "that I have ever
known a purer or more benevolent man, — a man for
whose integrity and uprightness I have entertained
a more profound respect." His circle of warm-
hearted friends was somewhat extensive. His acquaintance was deservedly sought; his presence imparted intelligence and pleasure to every circle in
which he moved. He evidently lived not for himself,
but for the good of his generation. He uniformly
aimed to diffuse happiness around him. Without
the prospect of reward in the present life, he was
sustained and animated with the hope of a reward
in the world to come. Upon that reward for which

his Lord had so manifestly been preparing him for a long course of years, he has no doubt, through grace, joyfully entered. And hundreds and hundreds, who have enjoyed his society and shared in his labors for their benefit, now "rise up and call him blessed."

At a meeting of the alumni of Williams College, held August, 1863, — thirty years after the death of Dr. Fitch, — it was decided to erect a monument to his memory on this spot — the principal scene of his successful and useful labors. The work was intrusted to the Executive Committee, who were also requested, if possible, to procure a portrait.* Liberally aided by Dr. S. S. Fitch, of New York, the committee found no difficulty in securing from a few of the alumni the necessary funds, — five hundred and fifty dollars. The monument (made in Pittsfield) has two plinths or bases, the lower one four feet square, with a die or main pillar, surmounted by a handsome urn, — the whole about fourteen feet high, and weighing six and a half tons. It was erected in the college cemetry, on the last of June, 1864, and bears the following inscriptions : —

---

* In addition to his liberal contribution toward the monument, and his aid in publishing the sketch of President Fitch, the alumni are now to be indebted to the liberality of Dr. S. S. Fitch for a large and well-executed portrait of his worthy uncle. No reasonable pains or expense have been spared to procure one that shall be correct and acceptable.

[On the West side.]

IN MEMORY OF

REV. EBENEZER FITCH, D. D.

FIRST PRESIDENT OF WILLIAMS
COLLEGE,

Born at Norwich, Ct.,

SEPT. 26, 1756;

GRADUATED AT YALE COLLEGE, 1777,

TUTOR THERE 8 YEARS.

BECAME PRECEPTOR OF

THE ACADEMY AT WILLIAMSTOWN,

OCT., 1790.

PRESIDENT OF THE COLLEGE, 1793;

RESIGNED THE PRESIDENCY

1 8 1 5;

INSTALLED AT WEST BLOOMFIELD, N. Y.,

NOV. 29, 1815.

RESIGNED NOV. 25, 1827.

DIED THERE MARCH 21, 1833,

AGED 76 YEARS.

[On the North side.]

PRÆS. FITCH RELIQUIÆ

AD OPPID. GUL. ALLATÆ SUNT,

ET HOC MONUMENTUM ERECTUM EST

AB SUIS COGNATIS ET COLL GUL. ALUMNIS,

ANNO 1864.

[On the South side.]

IN MEMORIAM

EBENEZER FITCH, D. D.

VIR CLARISSIMUS

DOCTRINA ET INDUSTRIA,

HUMANITATE ET PIETATE;

EJUS EXEMPLUM ET PRECEPTA

SUÆ ÆTATI PROFUERUNT,

ET FUTURIS TEMPORIBUS BENE FACIENT.

At the suggestion of some of Dr. Fitch's relatives, his remains (found in a good state of preservation) were removed from West Bloomfield, N. Y., to Williamstown ; and on Tuesday evening, July 5, 1864, immediately after prayers in the chapel, the Faculty and some of the Trustees, and other graduates and friends of the college, who were attending the senior examination, repaired to the college cemetery, and reverently consigned the honored remains to their new resting-place. The feelings prompted by the occasion found a fitting expression in the following remarks, made by the Hon. Judge Bishop, of Lenox : —

"In the little box around which we are standing are the ashes of an eminently good and useful man. They are all that remains on earth of him who first gave form and vitality to the institution whose buildings crown the elevations of this valley, and from which so many have gone out to enlighten and elevate mankind. Among those here, I am told, I am the only one who was a member of college during his presidency. Of his own and the succeeding generation, few remain. There are impressions made upon the heart which time cannot efface. The relics before us bring back again, in full force, the sentiments of reverence which the living presence inspired. I see his dignified form again, his grave and benignant features, his courteous demeanor, his happy smile, and feel again the veneration which the lapse of half a century has not extinguished. In September, 1814, I entered college. Dr. Fitch left it in September of the year following. I knew him only as a presiding officer. As such, he made the acquaintance of the students of the several classes. He regarded them as his children, and his government of them was that of a father. He was coercive, reluctantly and judiciously coercive,

when persuasive kindness failed, and only then. He mingled
with his pupils with cheerful, serene familiarity. His manners
were those which high attainments give to a good heart and refined breeding.

" He was a Christian gentleman. In the devotional exercises
of the college he was impressively earnest and solemn. The su-
premacy and authority of divine truths, as revealed, were earnestly enforced. No one who heard him discourse upon their relative importance will ever forget how he placed them high above
all scientific and literary attainments, and his urgent advocacy for
their diffusion throughout the world. He dwelt with peculiar
delight upon Christian missions, the good they had wrought, and
their prospects. Initiated by such a man, it is no wonder that
this college stands preëminent for its missionary zeal, — that
Mills, and Hall, and James Richards should have become what
they were, under the inspiring teachings of one so able and so
devoted to the spread of the gospel. The impress which he
made in this respect upon the college still lasts. This is most
obvious to those who knew it early and know it now. May the
mantle cast upon it by him whose bones are here, cover it forever !

" I have always regarded Dr. Fitch as the real founder of this
institution, — that had he not been, it would not have existed as
it now does. He came here early, — a ripe scholar, apt, and
eminently qualified to teach. He was thoroughly equal to
impart all that an education then thought liberal required. No
collegiate institution was near ; increasing population and intelligence demanded one. He was qualified to supervise and control it. The materials for its inception were at hand. He suggested their use, and, in a good measure, directed their application. May he not, therefore, be permitted to share, without im-
pairing, the just fame of him whose munificence is acknowledged
by the name with which the institution has been christened ?

" I retain with a good degree of distinctness the impression
which his preaching made upon my mind, and the characteristics
of his eloquence. His sermons were no academic discourses, pol-

ished and elaborate, of lofty style and glowing imagery, challenging for the speaker the admiration of his audience. He spoke for truth's sake, not for his own. He loved the truth better than he loved himself. He preached it, that others might be brought to love it. This was the end of his preaching. To that end all his forces were directed. His sermons were full of the deep sensibilities of his own pure and affectionate nature, made active by the clear conviction of the truths which he enforced. He seemed impressed with the belief that his audience were to be influenced and drawn to the truth through the affections, — that, the heart once touched, the reason ceases to cavil, and the will becomes submissive. In a word, his was the eloquence of Christian love, purifying all that is tender, affectionate, and holy in the heart.

"To you, sir, whose active and disinterested devotion to the college, founded in no small measure by the good and learned man whose name and deeds we hope to perpetuate, I tender my cordial thanks and congratulations. You have brought from a distance, to be buried here amidst the scenes of his usefulness, all that is material which is left of him. We now bury 'these sacred relics' at the foot of the very appropriate monumental marble which you have caused to be erected, and on which you have written his name and character. This was due to his memory, to the college whose first president he was, and is worthy of one enrolled among her steadfast and devoted sons.

"In the name of the few surviving pupils of President Fitch, I thank you for this manifestation of your appreciation of his worth, and recognition of his eminent services in the cause of science, humanity, and Christian civilization."

11

A DISCOURSE

ADDRESSED TO THE CANDIDATES FOR THE BACCALAUREATE
IN WILLIAMS COLLEGE, SEPTEMBER 1, 1799. BY THE REV.
EBENEZER FITCH, PRESIDENT OF WILLIAMS COLLEGE.

"Covet earnestly the best gifts; and yet show I unto you a more excellent way."
— 1 Corinthians xii. 31.

HE Christian philosopher often contemplates, with pleasing astonishment, the works of God. Their number, variety, properties, powers, and uses excite his admiration of the divine wisdom. The goodness displayed in their formation, in their fitness for the ends intended, and capacities for enjoyment, calls forth his gratitude and praise. But man, the last and noblest piece of divine workmanship in this world, claims the greatest share of his attention. He sees him to be distinguished, in several important respects, from the inferior orders of animals. *Their* powers are very limited, and admit of little enlargement or improvement; *his* may be improved and enlarged almost to infinity. *Their* capacities for enjoyment are scanty, and admit only the low, gross pleasures of sense; *his* are large, highly improvable, and

(122)

fitted for the noblest intellectual and moral pleasures. Distinguished as man is from the inferior orders of creatures, is it not strange that any, boasting of high claims to reason and philosophy, should be so brutish as to suppose him destined to the same common lot, — to perish forever, and be forgotten? Reason and revelation concur in their decision, that he has a far higher and nobler destiny. The breath of the Almighty has made him immortal, and given him powers capable of endless progressive improvement in knowledge and virtue, and capacities for commensurate enjoyment of the purest intellectual and moral kind.

But the mental powers and faculties of man were not made to grow, like vegetables, or animal bodies, without any labor or exertion of his own. They need diligent culture, vigorous exercise, the aids of science, and the benign influence of religion, to bring them to maturity. The understanding must be enlarged, strengthened, and enriched with knowledge, and the will and affections amended, regulated, and improved by virtue. The cultivation of the heart should keep pace with the growth and enlargement of the mental powers. Intellectual endowments, natural or acquired, can never alone raise man to that elevated rank in the scale of being which his Maker designed him to hold. Virtue and religion must unite their happifying and ennobling influence to raise him to the true dignity of a rational, immortal creature. " Covet earnestly," says the apostle, "the best gifts; and yet show I unto you a more excellent way."

On this occasion, young gentlemen, the last I ever expect of speaking to you publicly as a class, I feel it to be my duty to address you with the freedom of a friend, and with the seriousness and engagedness becoming a minister of Christ. To impress on your minds some of the interesting truths suggested in the text, I shall endeavor, in the first place, to show you that there are some gifts which are highly valuable, and worthy your diligent pursuit, and point out some of the ways in which they may be improved; secondly, to suggest some motives which ought to influence you to the diligent pursuit and faithful improvement of them; and, thirdly, to make it evident that there is a still more excellent and important way.

In the first place, I am to show you that some gifts are highly valuable, and worthy your diligent pursuit, and point out some of the ways in which they may be improved. Gifts, talents, or powers, are natural, supernatural, or acquired. Natural gifts or talents, though capable of being increased and improved, and applied to valuable purposes, cannot be objects of pursuit. They are such as God, their author, has been pleased to make them. Thus, one man has a gift or talent which enables him to excel in one walk of science, one art or profession, and another in another. He who has not one of these gifts can never acquire it by any labor, study, or ex-

ertion. " *Poeta nascitur, non fit*," * said the Romans ;
and the same observation is equally applicable to
every natural gift or talent.

There are also supernatural gifts. Of these the
apostle had been particularly speaking in the preceding context. These were the gifts of miracles,
of prophesying, of healing the sick, and of speaking
or interpreting an unknown language. Among the
primitive Christians, many, by the immediate agency of the divine Spirit, were endowed with these ex-
traordinary, miraculous gifts. They answered, at
that day, the important purpose of facilitating and
expediting the spread of the gospel among rude,
unenlightened, idolatrous nations. God by them
bore testimony to the doctrines of the cross, in a
manner calculated to silence the cavils of unbeliev-
ing Jews, and bring conviction to the minds of ignorant Gentiles. But the reasons for bestowing
these miraculous gifts on the ministers of religion
long since generally ceased, and with them the gifts
themselves. It does not appear, therefore, that it is
now the duty of Christians to pray for them, or
desire them.

Acquired gifts, or talents, are those of which I
mean principally to treat, and which I would recommend as objects worthy your diligent and strenuous
pursuit.

Science or knowledge, extensively considered, is

---

* A man is *born*, and not *made*, a poet.

11*

a gift or talent of general use and application. It is, in ten thousand different ways, conducive to the improvement and happiness of man. Without it, he would still be a savage, elevated by his natural powers only above the brutal herd. All the refinements of society, all its accommodations and elegant delights, owe their origin to science. Contrast the condition of savages with that of civilized nations, and see the striking difference. View, if you can, without the mingled emotions of astonishment and pleasure, the benefits resulting to individuals and society from the cultivation of the human mind, and the treasures of knowledge with which it has been stored. To recount them all would be a task as difficult and endless as to number the stars, or tell the sands on the sea-shore. Many of them, in a highly improved state of society, are, like air and light, so common as hardly to be noticed. We see and feel and enjoy them, without considering from what source they spring, or reflecting that they are not natural or incidental.

Philology, or the knowledge of language, is valuable, principally, as the means or instrument either of acquiring or communicating other knowledge, and as the medium of social intercourse. Endowed by our beneficent Creator with the faculty of speech, it becomes us to improve it, as the means, not merely of interchanging our thoughts in the common concerns of life, but of communicating to each other the knowledge of him and his works. The man

who becomes eminent in the use of this faculty ac-
quires a commanding influence over the opinions,
passions, and actions of his fellow-men. He has it
in his power, not merely to please, instruct, and per-
suade, but to convince, arouse, animate, impel.
Paul of Tarsus was celebrated, even by the learned
heathen of that day, as one of the first orators of
the age. And to what a noble purpose was his oratory applied! Thousands now in heaven, converted
under his preaching from gross ignorance and idolatry, or an obstinate and blind attachment to Juda-
ism, can testify, and will testify forever.

Need I undertake to point out to you, young gentlemen, the numerous inferior advantages and uses
of oratory? Is it not one of the first qualifications,
one of the most brilliant ornaments of the lawyer
and the statesman, as well as of the divine? Diligently cultivate, then, this talent; earnestly covet
this highly valuable and useful gift.

Were it, on this occasion, proper, I might proceed
to recommend to your diligent and persevering pursuit every branch of useful knowledge. I might
mention the many advantages derived from a knowledge of this terraqueous globe, its numerous and
various inhabitants, their manners, laws, history,
forms of government, civil, literary, and religious institutions. I might eulogize the benefits resulting
from natural science, and invite you to examine,
with philosophic care and accuracy, and contem-
plate, with devout admiration, the various produc-

tions of infinite skill, power, and benevolence in this material world. I might show you how such researches invigorate the powers of the mind, enlarge the bounds of knowledge, contribute to the convenience, accommodation, and happiness of man, and raise his views to that Almighty Being who called the world into existence, and who superintends, regulates, and controls all the operations of this vast and complicated machine. In short, I might undertake to point out to you all the various uses and advantages of the knowledge of those arts and sciences which compose a course of liberal education, and which have engaged so large a share of your attention during your academic life. But, pleasing as would be the task, I must waive it for one more important and better suited to the occasion.

General science, as was observed, is a talent or gift of extensive application and utility. The man whose mind is enriched with every kind of knowledge can, as occasion may require, bring out of his treasure things new and old. He has in himself, whether alone or in company, a fund of rational pleasure. He can entertain and instruct the listening circle, and shed on all around him the light of wisdom and knowledge. In how many ways, and to how great an extent, may he be useful to his fellow-men? If he is disposed to improve his knowledge for the good of others, he is the blessing and the ornament of society. What a debt of gratitude is due to men of such eminent erudition as Bacon

and Boyle and Newton and Locke! And, to
the honor of human nature, we might add to this
list a long catalogue of names truly illustrious in
the republic of letters.

But, to become eminent for general knowledge,
great abilities, much leisure, long and close application are requisite. Few, therefore, shine as general
scholars, while many figure in some particular department of science. That knowledge is always
most valuable which is most useful. That which is
most directly applicable to the common occasions
and occupations of life merits your first attention
All that knowledge, especially, which conduces to
extensive usefulness in professional life, should be
eagerly sought by youth who design to engage in
the learned professions. It becomes, in their hands,
a gift or talent of constant, daily use. The mere
scholar, the man of idle speculation, who pursues
his researches in science solely for the purpose of
gratifying his taste or curiosity, or acquiring fame,
is a useless drone in society. It should always be
your aim to improve your knowledge for some valuable purpose.

To men of education, the learned professions
open the fairest and largest field for usefulness. To
figure and be useful in either of them, much particular knowledge must be added to the general stock.
When, by a course of laborious study, you have
made this addition, you will possess a gift or talent

which may be employed to great advantage for the good of mankind.

To relieve the pains and heal the maladies to which our frail bodies are subject is an important and benevolent office. Our compassionate Saviour often discharged it; not, indeed, as an ordinary, but as an almighty physician. He did not deem even the hours of the Sabbath too sacred to be employed in this friendly and necessary duty. All the individual happiness consequent upon the continuance of life and the enjoyment of health, and all the benefits thence resulting to others, may, and often do, depend, under God, upon the seasonable, judicious, and skilful application of the healing art. Let, then, those who would, in this way, be eminent and useful, diligently seek and benevolently improve this gift.

In every society laws are necessary to regulate the civil conduct of individuals. As men and as Christians, we all have important rights which we wish to enjoy, and which duty requires us to protect and defend. Till that happy, promised period shall arrive, when fraud and injustice, theft and violence, adultery and murder, with every other species of wickedness, shall cease, our property, our rights, and our lives will need the protection of wise and salutary laws, executed with firmness and impartial justice. A thorough knowledge of these laws, in the present highly improved state of society, has become an arduous and important study. To understand them in their true spirit and principle, explain them clearly, and apply them with precision and justice, constitutes the business of a useful and necessary profession. If to your fund of general knowledge you add the hard-earned treasures of juridical science, you will have a gift or talent which, if used with honor and integrity, will procure you wealth and reputation, and be of essential service to your fellow-men. It will, also, furnish you with still greater gifts, and fit you for a higher station and more extensive usefulness in the departments of civil life.

But the gift most to be desired, because it may be applied to the highest and noblest purpose, is to be exercised in another profession. Men have not only temporal, but eternal interests to be advanced and promoted by the labors of the learned, the virtuous, and the pious. As much as the soul in native dignity and worth surpasses the body, as much as eternity exceeds time in duration, so much do the interests of a future life exceed in importance those of the present. Our pain or pleasure in this life is, at most, slight and momentary; but, in the life to come, one or the other will be exquisite and endless. God, whose all-comprehending view takes in at once the whole of our existence, with all our concerns and interests, has shown us by his conduct, in a manner more convincing and impressive, if possible, than the strongest declarations in his word, the importance of our well-being in the life

to come. Though he has not been unmindful of
our present felicity, he appears unspeakably more
solicitous about our future welfare. He has been,
if I may so say, at infinite trouble and expense to
rescue us from misery, and procure us happiness in
the coming world. We are redeemed, not by cor-
ruptible things, as silver and gold, but by the precious blood of the Son of God. This was the infinite price paid for our salvation. Had all the angels in heaven died for us, it would have availed
nothing. Divine justice demanded an infinite ran-
som. The death of the great Emmanuel alone
could be accepted as an adequate atonement for the
guilt of fallen man. Such was the evil of sin, and
such the worth of the soul in the view of omni-
science! Through Christ's atoning blood, pardon,
peace, and eternal life are tendered to guilty men.
The divine Saviour himself proclaimed the joyful
news of this great salvation, and appointed in his
church an order of men, to be continued in every
successive age, whose business it is to publish the
same glad tidings. They are his ambassadors,
commissioned to proclaim the terms of peace and
reconciliation to a world in arms against him, their
rightful Sovereign. High and honorable is their office; solemn and interesting are the duties and services it requires. These ministers of the Prince of
Peace need all the aids of human learning, as well
as the teachings of his Spirit, to qualify them for
their important trust. All who desire this office

should earnestly covet these gifts. They should not be novices, lest they be elevated with pride, and fall into the snare of the tempter. Their divine Master directs them " to be wise as serpents, though harmless as doves." They must be able, by sound doctrine, to stop the mouths of gainsayers, to instruct the ignorant, support the weak, reclaim the erroneous, console the afflicted, raise up the desponding, and animate the drooping Christian; to reprove, rebuke, exhort, with all long-suffering, meekness, and wisdom. To do all this, and much more, which the important duties of their sacred office require, is a task too arduous for any man who is not enlightened by the Spirit of God, aided by his grace, and assisted by all the helps of human learning. In no other business or calling is it so necessary that a man should be a *scholar* as well as a Christian. Useful knowledge, then, is a gift of high importance to the minister of Christ. He should covet and seek this knowledge earnestly, as one of the best acquirable gifts. While young, especially, he should spare no pains, labor, or study to possess it, and should make it the business and pleasure of his life to employ it diligently, with all his other gifts, in promoting the divine glory, and the immortal interests of his fellow-men. I proceed,

Secondly, to suggest some motives which ought to influence you to the diligent pursuit and faithful improvement of these gifts.

Permit me, in the first place, to suggest as a motive, your own interest and reputation. In the course of your collegiate life, you have acquired a considerable stock of useful knowledge. This is not only valuable in itself, but it will enable you, with greater ease and expedition, to make large additions. It is a broad and solid foundation, on which a noble and elegant superstructure may be erected. The road to the temple of Science is now open before you. Most of the obstructions are removed. You have progressed in it a considerable way. Will you stop here, and proceed no farther in a path which conducts directly to honor and usefulness? Would this be reputable? Would it comport with your interests? If you love books, you will make them the companions of all your leisure hours. If you desire knowledge, you will seek it as silver, and search for it as for hid treasures. You will not rest satisfied with present literary attainments, but labor, as you have leisure and opportunity, to acquire more knowledge, and to become eminent for science. To this both interest and reputation strongly prompt you, as they do also to a diligent and faithful improvement of your gifts, whether natural or acquired. By these you hope to procure for yourselves the supports, comforts, accommodations, and, perhaps, elegancies of life. By a right use of these, you may merit and obtain the good opinion, if not the applause, of men.

I may suggest, as a second motive, the just and reasonable expectation of your friends. Great have been their care and solicitude for your progress in knowledge, and perseverance in a course of virtuous conduct. Your parents and friends have been at no small expense to give you the advantages of a collegiate education. They have raised expectations of finding that you have greatly profited by these advantages, that you will do honor to yourselves and to them, and be blessings and ornaments to society. Can you bear the idea of disappointing their well-founded hopes? Do not the sentiments of honor, of filial affection, duty and gratitude, glow in your bosoms, and inspire you with a resolution to be and to do all, and more, if possible, than they expect? This is the best, if not the only way, in your power to make them suitable and acceptable returns for all their care and anxiety, expense and trouble. You never can know, till you are parents yourselves, the feelings of a parent's heart. His solicitude for the preservation, improvement, reputation, temporal prosperity, and eternal welfare of his offspring often exceeds your conception. Tremblingly alive to everything that nearly concerns them, he spares no pains, he grudges no expense, to fit them to be useful, respectable, and virtuous members of society. Think of this, my young friends, and let an equal solicitude possess your minds, and influence you to everything useful, laudable, and virtuous.

A third motive, which I would urge, is the just claim which society has to the labors and services of men of education. "That we are born, not for ourselves, but for our country," was the noble sentiment of a heathen. Shall not Christians think as nobly? Shall the man rich in knowledge hoard his treasure as the miser does his gold? Shameful selfishness! What! Have stores of knowledge, which cannot be diminished by communication nor exhausted by distribution, and yet not communicate nor distribute! And this, too, when so much good may be done ; when so many may be made wiser, and better, and happier by the means! Forbid it honor, patriotism, piety! Talents for usefulness should not be buried in a napkin. To whom much is given, of them much is required, both by God and their country. Countless are the ways in which your gifts may be employed for the public good. Men of abilities, science, and virtue easily acquire influence. They can do much for the encouragement of learning, true patriotism, and good morals, which are all highly important, as they are necessary to the support of social order, good government, and religion. In this day, especially, of general and alarming danger, when every civil and religious institution is threatened with ruin, when a spirit of vandalism, hostile to rational liberty, and to everything dear to us as men and Christians, has already devastated the fairest parts of Europe, and menaces the civilized world with universal carnage, rapine, and desolation, every man of science, every friend to virtue and his country, is called upon to exert every nerve to stem the raging torrent. You cannot innocently remain idle spectators of the awful catastrophe of nations, the prostration of all good government, and the extirpation of morality and religion from the earth. All this, and more, appears evidently to be comprised in the infernal plan of the combined atheists and revolutionists of the present day. Witness their dark conspiracies, now brought to light, their daring, persevering, and deadly efforts, nay, their own direct and positive declarations. Stand, then, at your posts, and die like men, rather than suffer that liberty for which our fathers bled, that government which they established with so much wisdom, and that religion which they held dearer than life, to be sacrificed at the unhallowed shrine of atheism and French philosophy. Let the sticklers for this philosophy deny that religion and government are in danger from a combination of men desperate in wickedness, and prepared for every enormity. With the same modest assurance they may deny that the sun enlightens the world. Your information is such that their confident denial cannot, in the least degree, shake your belief. You know that the world is now in possession of the fullest evidence of this unhappy and alarming fact. You know that, not only in Europe, but in our own enlightened country, the principles of deism, atheism, and disorganizing politics, have, of late years, made rapid strides. Is no danger to be apprehended from such principles? Do they not sap the pillars

12*

of society? Are not many well-meaning but unin-
formed persons, by the wicked arts of ambitious
men, drawn into the vortex of these principles, and
marshalled on the side of opposition to the wisest
and best government on the globe? While you
hold the vile arts of such deceivers in abhorrence,
pity even the willing victims of their sophistry and
falsehood. Labor to enlighten, undeceive, and convince them. Obstinate as many of them are in
their prejudices and opinions, possibly truth and
reason may at length prevail, and triumph over their
errors and delusion. God, in his kind providence, is
now opening the eyes of some of them. He appears,
also, to be turning the scale against the enemies of religion and rational liberty in Europe. But the same
abominable and ruinous principles are likely long to
ferment in the bosom of society, and endanger the
existence of everything dear and valuable to men
and to Christians. Great care and circumspection,
vigorous and unceasing exertions, will still be required of the friends of God and their country, to
guard against the fatal tendency of these principles,
and secure mankind from their pernicious effects.
Let your learning, patriotism, and piety be employed
for this important and benevolent purpose.

From you, young gentlemen, society claims many
other services. Time does not allow me to enumer-
ate them. Most of them your own reflections will
readily suggest. There is, however, one highly important kind of service, which a sense of duty for-

bids me to omit. This extensive and growing
country is at present in great need of religious instructors. Many of our old towns, and a great
number of our new settlements, have none to break
to them the bread of life. A plentiful harvest of
souls is in danger of being lost for want of laborers.
Does not the cry of many "ready to perish" ring in
your ears, and call you to the vineyard? If wealth
and fame do not await you, in this sacred employment, the blessings of perishing immortals will come
upon you, and a crown of glory be your eternal reward. How important is it to the civil and literary
interest of society, as well as to the immortal welfare of the souls of men, that all should have the
benefit of religious instruction! Ignorance, immor-
ality, and impiety will, otherwise, soon prevail, and
envelop our land in the darkness of heathenism.
Our wise and free government will be prostrated in
the dust, anarchy will succeed, and despotism close
the tragic scene. Our religion — the pure and holy
religion of the gospel — will be exchanged for the
dark, chaotic systems of infidelity, or the gloomy
horrors of annihilation and atheism. But, blessed
be God! we entertain better hopes respecting our
government and our religion. Jehovah reigns! He
will defend his own cause. He will protect his
church. Against it the gates of hell shall not ultimately prevail. We have many favorable tokens of
his presence and protection in the effusions of his
Spirit on many places, in the continuance of wise

and upright men to be our rulers, and in the general superintendence of his kind providence over all our national concerns.

I will suggest but one motive more, and that is of the highest moment, and ought to have the most persuasive and commanding influence. God claims your best services. They are justly and unalienably his due. All your powers and faculties, your talents and opportunities for usefulness, should be devoted to him. He is served, his glory is promoted, when, with upright views, you labor to advance the happiness of his creatures. Unprofitableness is inexcusable and criminal. To neglect the improvement of the talents he has given you is ingratitude and disobedience. Your being, your powers, your advantages for education, and the knowledge you have acquired, are all his gifts, and he justly requires that you employ them for his glory. The period allotted you for active usefulness is short, but the consequences, to yourselves and to others, of improving or neglecting it, will run through eternity. Let these and similar considerations animate you to diligence, zeal, and faithfulness in the discharge of every personal, social, and religious duty.

I am, thirdly, to show you that however desirable and worthy of pursuit the best gifts may be, there is still a more excellent and glorious way. This is the way of holiness, which leads directly and certainly to present peace and future happiness. Talents without piety, gifts without grace, will not profit you at last. Splendid abilities may dazzle the eyes of men, and command their admiration and applause. But true virtue alone can procure the divine favor, and insure the rewards of a better life. This alone gives real worth and importance to genius and erudition, to brilliant talents and extensive knowledge. What do wit, genius, and learning now avail Hume and Bolingbroke, Shaftesbury and Voltaire? Prostituted as these talents were by them to the infamous cause of infidelity and vice, what purpose do they now answer but as flaming torches to light them to the lowest pits of their infernal prison, and show them, in tenfold horrors, the regions of eternal darkness? What would they now give for one cheering ray of that heavenly religion which they hooted and despised? — for one drop of His atoning blood, whom, with the rage and malice of fiends, they so often reviled and blasphemed?

You, my young friends, have formed, I trust, a more just estimate of the worth of religion. But its real value cannot, in the present state, be fully told or conceived. When the splendors of eternal day shall burst upon your astonished sight, or the pit of endless despair yawn before you, then, and not till then, will you know its infinite worth, its high and everlasting importance. Enough, however, is now known to convince every rational man that to possess and practise it is his highest interest, as well as his indispensable duty. This is that wisdom which is "the principal thing," both for present enjoyment and future felicity. All her ways are pleasantness, all her paths are peace, and her rewards are glory, honor, and immortality. Let, then, this heavenly wisdom be your companion and your guide through the world, upon the broad theatre of which you are now entering. Act well the various parts which Providence may assign you. As you will leave behind you a fair reputation for laudable progress in science, and for orderly and amiable deportment, preserve and increase this reputation by future diligence, usefulness, and virtue. Think often on what you owe to yourselves and to your friends, to your country and your God. Labor more to be virtuous than to be learned, — to be good than to be great. Value less the applause of men than the testimony of a good conscience, and the approbation of your Maker.

We commend you to the grace, protection, and blessing of Almighty God. May he direct you in all your ways, improve you as instruments of great good to men and glory to his name, make you blessings to your friends, your country, and the world, and, at last, crown your faithful and benevolent services here with immortal glory and felicity in the world above. Amen.

A SERMON

DELIVERED BEFORE THE MISSIONARY SOCIETY OF BERKSHIRE
AND COLUMBIA, AT THEIR ANNUAL MEETING, IN HUDSON, N.
Y., SEPTEMBER 20, 1814. BY EBENEZER FITCH, D. D., PRES-
IDENT OF WILLIAMS COLLEGE.

"For the weapons of our warfare are not carnal, but mighty through God to the
pulling down of strong-holds." — 2 CORINTHIANS, x. 4.

AUL was honored by God as the founder of the Corinthian Church. Apollos, Silvanus, Timotheus, and others, labored with him in watering it, and building it up in the faith and order of the gospel. Under their ministry it soon became a numerous and flourishing church. But false teachers crept in, and endeavored to alienate the minds of the brethren from their spiritual fathers and teachers. Their wicked endeavors were so far successful as to produce very unhappy contentions and divisions, and cause Paul's claim to the apostleship to be called in question. They reviled him, and affected to despise him for his smallness of stature, his humble appearance, and unassuming deportment. "His bodily presence," said they, "is weak, and his speech contemptible."

(143)

Some years before, when, in the presence of Felix
and Drusilla, he reasoned of righteousness, temperance, and judgment to come, Felix trembled. And
two years after this, when he made his very able
and eloquent defence before Festus and Agrippa,
they felt and acknowledged the power of his eloquence. Longinus speaks of him as one of the first
orators of antiquity. But it is evident that when he
preached at Corinth he was no longer distinguished
as an orator. The ecstasy, or trance, mentioned in
the twelfth chapter of this epistle, when he was
caught up to the third heaven, and heard unspeakable words, might have so affected his nerves as to
injure the organs of speech, and produce a lasting
impediment. It is no improbable conjecture that
such an impediment was " the thorn in the flesh, the
messenger of Satan sent to buffet him, lest he should
be exalted above measure." " For this thing," said
he, " I besought the Lord thrice, that it might depart from me. And he said unto me, ' My grace is
sufficient for thee ; for my strength is made perfect
in weakness.' " God probably intended it should
fully appear that the vicious and idolatrous Gentiles were not converted by the conclusive reasoning
and persuasive eloquence of Paul, but by the power
and grace of his Spirit. That this was the fact, Paul
appeals to the Corinthians themselves in his first
epistle. " And I, brethren, when I came to you,
came not with excellency of speech, or of wisdom.
And I was with you in weakness, and in fear, and

in much trembling.   And my speech and my preaching was not with enticing words of man's wisdom,
but in demonstration of the Spirit and of power:
that your faith should not stand in the wisdom of
men, but in the power of God." The same sentiment appears in the words chosen for our text.
" The weapons of our warfare," saith the apostle,
" are not carnal, but mighty through God to the
pulling down of strong-holds."

These words naturally lead us to consider the following things : —

I.   The means employed in the propagation of
the gospel.

II.   The great Agent who gives efficacy to these
means; and,

III.   The effects produced.

We are first to consider the means employed in
the propagation of the gospel.

When Christ was about to enter upon his public
ministry, he sent a herald before him to prepare the
way.   John the Baptist came, as Isaiah and Mala-
chi had foretold, preaching in the wilderness of Judea, and saying, " Repent ye; for the kingdom of
heaven is at hand." When John's short ministry
terminated in his imprisonment by Herod, Christ
himself appeared as a public teacher.   The Spirit
of the Lord was eminently upon him, because he
had anointed him to preach the gospel to the poor,
he had sent him to heal the broken-hearted, to
preach deliverance to the captives, and recovery of

13

sight to the blind. He, indeed, spake as never man
spake, and evinced his Messiahship by a series of
the most benevolent and stupendous miracles. But
when, by his death and resurrection, his mediatorial
work on earth was fully accomplished, to whom did
he commit the prosecution of his great design of
instructing, reforming, and saving an ignorant, apostate, perishing world of sinners? Did he commit
this immense and godlike work to mighty princes
and potentates at the head of armies and nations;
or to great, wise, and learned sages and philoso-
phers? Such a measure human policy — the wisdom of this world — would probably have dictated.
But the divine Saviour, who perfectly knew the
hearts of men, the state of the world, and the work
to be accomplished, chose very different instruments.
During his public ministry he selected twelve plain,
illiterate men as his constant attendants, to receive
his instructions, imbibe his doctrines, and be witnesses of his miracles. To these men he committed
the work of publishing his gospel through the world,
— of instructing, and reclaiming from error, prejudice,
and sin, millions of Jews and Gentiles. This was
their commission: " *Go ye into all the world, and
preach the gospel to every creature.*" Was ever so
arduous a task assigned to men? Did God ever
require any of his creatures to perform a work so laborious, so difficult, and, to human strength, so impossible? Yet they undertook it, and accomplished
it, in a way which fully accorded with the purpose

and requirement of God. And by what means did
they accomplish it? Certainly not by human power or policy. Not by the aid of eminent natural
abilities, learning, or eloquence. They possessed
none of these,—they used none of these. They were
a small, feeble band of plain, unlettered men. They
stood alone, unaided, unbefriended by any human
power, civil or ecclesiastical. Nay, all the world
was in hostile array against them. The Jewish rulers, priests, and people, aided by the Roman arm,
had just crucified their Lord and Master. All the
supposed interests, all the religious and political
prejudices, and all the jealousies and passions of
that disappointed nation united in rejecting his
claim to be their Messiah, and in despising and per-
secuting his followers. They had, therefore, nothing
but ill-will, contempt, persecution, and death to expect from their own countrymen if they adhered to
Christ's cause, and endeavored to propagate his
religion. Nor, if they turned from the Jews, and attempted to carry the glad tidings of salvation to the
Gentiles, was their prospect of safety and success,
to human appearance, less gloomy and discourag-
ing. Prejudices equally strange and numerous
were to be overcome, difficulties equally formidable
to be surmounted, and equal if not greater dangers
to their persons and lives to be apprehended. To encounter all this host of difficulties and dangers, and
accomplish the great object of their mission, what
were their means? What was their defensive ar-

mor, and what were their offensive weapons? The
apostle assures us they were not *carnal.* All the
powers of reason and eloquence could not remove
the prejudices of one Jew, and bring him cordially
to own and receive the despised and crucified Jesus
of Nazareth as his Messiah. Nor could they per-
suade one Gentile to abandon his idols and his sins,
believe in a crucified and risen Saviour, and worship
the only true God. Yet multitudes, both of Jews
and Gentiles, discarded all their deep-rooted prejudices, laid aside their hostility to Christ, embraced
the self-denying doctrines of his gospel, and not
only became his humble followers, but zealously labored in his cause, and patiently and nobly suffered
for his sake. How was all this effected? By what
the wise men of this world, as the apostle informs
us, were pleased to call, *the foolishness of preaching.*
Paul was the only one of the apostles who, as far as
we know, possessed any considerable share of learning or eloquence. And yet he informs us that Christ
sent him to preach the gospel, not with wisdom of
words, not with plausible reasonings, rhetorical
flourishes, and the arts of Grecian or Roman eloquence; but in plain, unadorned language, lest the
cross of Christ should be made of no effect. With
great plainness of speech, he presented the important doctrines and duties of the gospel to the understanding and the conscience. His message to man
was solemn and interesting, and he was aware that
no decorations of oratory could give such energy to

his doctrine, and bring truth so powerfully home to
the conscience and the heart, as to produce lasting
and saving effects. His aim and his practice was,
by plain and faithful preaching, in demonstration of
the spirit and of power, to commend himself to every
man's reason and conscience, in the sight of God.
This preaching was the means of awakening and
saving thousands. The stupid and thoughtless were
aroused from death-like sleep to a sense of their awful danger, the consciences of old and hardened sinners were appalled, and they cried out, " What must
we do to be saved?" Trembling, humbled peni-
tents were comforted, and hope divine sprang up in
their despairing, sinking souls, and believers were
edified, encouraged, strengthened, animated, and
made to rejoice with joy unspeakable and full of
glory. The means employed to produce these happy effects were a plain, faithful, solemn exhibition
of evangelical doctrine and duty to the understanding and consciences of men. It pleased God,
saith the apostle, by the *foolishness of preaching*, to
save them that believe. This is the appointed
means; a God has ever honored and blest, and
will continue to honor and bless, the means which
his own infinite wisdom appointed. The treasure
of the gospel is committed to earthen vessels, — to
frail, feeble, perishable instruments, — to men of like
passions with others, conscious of many defects and
imperfections; destitute of those human accom-
plishments, great talents, learning, and eloquence,

13*

which the world admires; without wealth, authority, or powerful friends; exposed to all the infirmities
and temporal evils incident to men, — to scorn, deri-
sion, and abuse from the wicked, and but partially
freed from the Christian's greatest burden, — the
effects of indwelling sin. God could have commissioned angels to proclaim to man the glorious truths
of the gospel. Or he could have put this treasure
into more splendid vessels by sending the most eminent and admired, the most wise, learned, and eloquent of the sons of men, to instruct mankind and
carry to them the joyful and glorious news of salvation through the atoning blood of Immanuel.
But God designed that the honor of saving sinners
should not be given to any created instruments or
:agents, but wholly to himself; he designed that the
excellency of the power should fully appear to be ·
of God, and not of men.

We proceed briefly to consider,

II. The great Agent who gives efficacy to the
appointed means.

We have seen, my brethren, the ancient heresy of
Arius and the more modern one of Socinus revived
in Europe, and embraced by men eminent for talents and erudition. Not a few of the professed
friends and ministers of Christ in our own country
have fallen into these fundamental errors. They
have been left to believe a lie, to bring in damnable
heresies, even denying the Lord that bought them,
and, there is great reason to fear, are bringing upon

themselves and their followers swift and awful de-
struction. Denying the real divinity of the Son of
God, they are led to call in question every essential
doctrine of the gospel, and obscure its whole glory,
by the thick mists of dangerous and fatal error.
With the divinity of Christ, they, of course, deny
the personality and agency of the Holy Spirit. But,
my brethren, I trust none of you have so learned
Christ; if so be ye have heard him, and have been
taught by him as the truth is in Jesus. You believe, as the Scriptures plainly and abundantly teach,
that fallen men are so thoroughly depraved as to
have no moral goodness remaining in their hearts,
no principle of holy obedience and true benevolence, no supreme love to their Maker, or cordial
good-will to their neighbor. Nay, you believe, as
Scripture asserts, that " *the carnal mind is enmity
against God;* " that it is not subject — that, indeed,
it cannot be subject — to the divine law. You see
the declarations of Scripture fully and awfully veri-
fied in the condition of our apostate race in the
present age and in all past ages. You behold, indeed, the whole world lying in iniquity, forgetting
the Lord their Maker, casting his laws behind their
backs, and trampling his authority under their feet,
saying to him by their practice, if not by their
words, " *Depart from us ; we desire not the knowledge
of thy ways.*" The natural fruits and consequences
of this universal depravity you view with astonishment, in the total ignorance of the true God, the

gross superstition, the stupid idolatry and polythe-ism, and the shocking and enormous vices of the whole heathen world, ancient and modern. You behold the same bitter root of depravity producing, in abundance, its hateful and baneful fruit in every civilized, enlightened, Christian country on the globe. Nay, to come nearer home, you feel its ex-istence, and deplore its influence and effects in your own hearts.

Can all the fine moral precepts and learned dog-mas of philosophy reform a world so depraved and desperately wicked? Can even the most lucid and striking exhibition of divine truth, the zealous, pa-thetic, and powerful preaching of the word of life, unaccompanied by the influence of the Spirit of God, effect this great object? If we can rely on the declarations of Scripture and the testimony of experience, we know that even *this* will avail noth-ing without the powerful coöperating energy of the blessed Spirit. It is his important office, in the economy of redemption, to enlighten the under-standing and to renew and sanctify the heart. Nat-ural men are extremely ignorant about spiritual things. They have no proper knowledge of the real character of God. They see no beauty or glory in any of his perfections. Their understand-ing is darkened, saith the apostle, and they are alienated from the life of God through the igno-rance that is in them, because of the blindness of their heart. It is the office of the Spirit to dispel

ignorance and darkness from such benighted minds.
And in all cases of saving illumination, that God,
who commanded the light to shine out of darkness,
shines in their hearts, to give the light of the knowledge of the glory of God in the face of Jesus
Christ. Such divinely-illuminated souls are born
of the Spirit. They are renewed in knowledge after
the image of God. They have an unction from the
holy One. The Spirit has begun the blessed work of
sanctification in their hearts. And he assuredly will
carry it on — and he alone can carry it on — to
the day of the Lord Jesus.

Need I take up your time, my Christian friends
and brethren, in adducing passages of Scripture in
proof of a doctrine so abundantly taught in the Bible, and I trust so firmly believed by us all, as that
the Spirit of God alone gives saving efficacy to the
preaching of the word, and to all the other appointed means of grace? Hear only the assertion
of the great apostle of the Gentiles: "*I have
planted, Apollos watered, but God gave the increase.*"
If other proofs are required, they may easily be
found in declarations and examples both in the
Old Testament and the New. I will, therefore, de-
tain you no longer on this branch of our subject,
but proceed to consider, —

III. The effects produced, through the coöperating agency of the Spirit, by the means which God
appointed for the spread of the gospel.

These effects, my brethren, have been truly great

and glorious. They have astonished and delighted the friends of the Redeemer on earth, and have given unspeakable joy to the angelic choirs. Among them there is joy over *one* sinner that repenteth. And who can count the myriads of sinful men who, since our Saviour's ascension, have repented and gone to glory? Soon after that event, the Spirit, like a mighty, rushing wind, descended and rested on the disciples. And they were all filled with the Holy Ghost, and began to speak with other tongues as the Spirit gave them utterance. Immediately upon this, the preaching of the gospel, through the powerful influence of the Spirit, began to produce its happy and glorious effects in the hearts of men. Three thousand were that day converted, five thousand a few days after; daily additions were made to their number, and even multitudes, both of men and women, we are told, flocked to the Saviour, and found mercy and salvation. From Jerusalem, this blessed work soon spread to all the cities and villages of Judea, Galilee, and Samaria, and then to the Gentiles. During the lifetime of the apostles, a great proportion of the heathen throughout the vast Roman empire, and some beyond its limits, heard the word of life preached, and multitudes of them forsook their idols, and became Christians. On every side the Redeemer extended and multiplied the triumphs of his cross, till, in less than three centuries from his ascension, Christianity, under Constantine the Great, became the religion of the whole Roman empire. The heathen idols had fallen before the banner of the cross, their temples were closed or demolished, their magistrates divested of power, and their oracles silenced. All this the apostles and their followers effected by the preaching of the gospel, accompanied by the powerful influences of the Spirit upon the hearts and consciences of men. So fully does it appear, as the apostle asserts in our text, "that the weapons of our warfare were not *carnal*, but *mighty* through God, to the pulling down of strong-holds." Satan had for ages been erecting, enlarging, and strengthening his strong-holds through the world. All the heathen nations had, for more than twenty centuries, "acknowledged his sway." This "prince of the power of the air" had reigned supreme in their hearts, had made them his willing captives, and led them blindfold at his pleasure, by millions and millions, to endless ruin. Except the Jews, not a nation or tribe was to be found on the earth that had not, from time immemorial, been the blind, zealous votaries of his cause, and the willing slaves of his power. We read in St. Luke that the seventy, whom Christ had sent forth to preach, returned again with joy, saying, "Lord, *even the devils are subject unto us through thy name.*" And he said unto them, "I beheld Satan as lightning fall from heaven." Thus *did* he fall, when his usurped dominion on earth, and the idolatrous worship he had established, were, in a sudden and surprising manner, by the preaching of the gospel, thrown down and destroyed.

Time will not permit me to trace the effects which the promulgation of the gospel produced, in different ages and countries, from Constantine to our day. Gloomy, indeed, was the state of Christianity through the greatest part of the intervening ages. While the man of sin — the apostate Bishop and Church of Rome — held their usurped dominion over the persons and consciences of men, and spread the dark cloud of their superstition and idolatry over the western Roman empire, a few, and but a few, real followers of the Lamb appeared to assert his cause. But at the era of the Reformation, the Saviour began again gloriously to triumph over the powers of darkness. Converts to the pure doctrine and practice of his gospel, from the dark recesses of Popish bigotry and superstition, were multiplied, and true religion again shed its benign influence on the hearts of individuals, and on the state of society. From that day to the present, notwithstanding the prevalence and reign of infidelity in some Christian countries, the trophies of the Redeemer have been numerous and increasing; and we have the strongest reasons, from prophecy and the intimations of Providence, to hope and believe that they will continue to increase, till all the nations of the earth shall flow unto Christ and be saved.

Having this hope, my brethren, are we to sit down, in a state of ease and indolence, to see the

progress of the Redeemer's cause, the gradual ex-
tension of his kingdom through the world? God
has ever employed instruments, human agents, his
ministers and people, to carry on his work, and by
their agency he *will continue* to carry it on. He is
indeed perfectly able to accomplish all his purposes
of mercy and grace to men without the intervention
of any instruments, means, or agents. He is rich in
mercy unto all that call upon him. And he has assured us that " Whosoever shall call upon the name
of the Lord shall be saved." But " how shall they
call on him in whom they have not believed?
and how shall they believe in him of whom they
have not heard? and how shall they hear without a
preacher?" As the preaching of the word is the appointed means to bring men to the knowledge of
God and Jesus Christ, the Saviour, — to the exercise
of faith in him, and salvation through his blood, —
our duty is plain. If we wish sinners to be saved,
we must send the gospel to them. This, my brethren, is the very object for which we have associated.
For this we are laboring, for this we are receiving
the charities of God's people, that we may hire
faithful laborers, and send them forth into the vineyard. And, surely, the faithful laborer in the vineyard of God is worthy of his hire. The Lord hath
ordained that they who preach the gospel should
live of the gospel. Missionaries to our infant settlements and to the heathen must receive aid and
support from us, or from similar societies of Chris-

14

tians. Many such societies have, within a few years, been formed in our country. And, blessed be God, he is opening the hearts of his people liberally to contribute of their abundance, for the accomplishment of their infinitely important and benevolent designs. I call their designs *infinitely* important and benevolent; and are they not indeed so? Who can estimate the worth of one soul? Shall we weigh in the balance against it the treasures of this, or of ten thousand worlds? The endless happiness of one immortal creature infinitely outweighs them all. Think of the millions of such creatures, now in our world, who are in the most imminent danger of perishing for lack of vision. The joyful sound of pardon and salvation through the merits of a bleeding Saviour has never reached them. They hardly know that there is a God to be worshipped, or a soul to be saved. If they acknowledge and worship any god, it is one which their own vain imaginations have conceived, and their own hands have formed, — a stock or a stone. They sit in darkness and in the shadow of death. No ray of gospel light has ever darted upon them from the Sun of righteousness. In vain is it to them that a Saviour has bled for guilty men, and that the Spirit of inspiration has dictated the volume of eternal truth, in which life and immortality are brought to light. They have never heard of this precious volume. They have never been told that they are sinners, and need a Saviour. They have no apprehension of what awaits them after death. If they attempt, with prying eyes, to look into the world beyond the grave, thick mists of impenetrable darkness wholly obstruct their view. Not a gleam of Christian hope gilds their path through life, or points them to a brighter world. And when death removes the veil, what astonishment, despair, and horror will seize them! View, my brethren, their present unhappy state, — consider for a moment the awful and end-less wretchedness that impends them; and if a spark of Christian compassion and benevolence is alive in your hearts, you will not only pity them and pray for them, but lift a vigorous arm to snatch them from eternal ruin. You will use your best and most strenuous endeavors to send heralds of peace and salvation to them, with the Word of Life in their hands. Your treasures of gold and silver will be opened, and you will, as the Lord enables you, cheerfully cast your free-will offering into his treasury, that his ambassadors of peace to the be-nighted and perishing nations of India, Africa, and the Isles may be refreshed on their way, and sup-ported in the arduous enterprise of carrying to them the glad tidings of salvation, and entreating them, in Christ's stead, to be reconciled to God.

Nor will you, my brethren, overlook the thousands of our fellow-citizens and countrymen, whose con-dition is scarcely less deplorable than that of the heathen. Doubtless many of my hearers have seen the report of the two young gentlemen, Messrs.

Mills and Schermerhorn, who, in 1812, "were employed by the Connecticut and Massachusetts Missionary Societies to make a tour through the southwestern parts of the United States, not only to preach as missionaries, but to gain information as to the state of religion in that immense tract of country." Their report exhibits a melancholy and painful view of the state of religion in those parts of our country and in the territories adjacent. Multitudes of immortal creatures in those extensive and thinly-settled regions are destitute of the means of religious instruction. So far from enjoying the stated ministration of the word, they seldom, if ever, hear a sermon from an itinerant preacher of any denomination. Nay, many of them have never seen the Bible, and have scarcely heard that there is a Saviour. Observing no Sabbath, without a Bible to read, or a minister to instruct them, they are sinking fast into a state of gross ignorance and vice approaching to heathenism. It is estimated that not less than two millions within the United States and their territories are in this deplorable condition. They are perishing by thousands, in this land of vision, for want of Bibles to read and ministers to preach to them the great and precious truths of the gospel, the unsearchable riches of Christ. Do not our hearts yearn over them? They are our countrymen, our brethren, our fellow-mortals. Their souls are as precious as our own. If our own salvation is of infinite importance, so also is theirs.

Has God furnished us with the means of sending the gospel to any of them; let us hasten to discharge this important duty, and, at the same time, lift up united and fervent cries to his throne, that he will accompany our endeavors with his blessing, and make the preaching of his word effectual to the salvation of multitudes ready to perish.

Great, my brethren, are the encouragements presented to us in his word and providence. Prophecies in abundance foretell the enlargement of the church, the prosperity of Zion, in the latter days. In these days we live. God is faithful; he will not suffer one iota to fail of all the great and glorious things which he has promised to his church. Christ must, and assuredly will, have the heathen for his inheritance, and the uttermost parts of the earth for his possession. All the ends of the earth will look unto him and be saved. The Jews will be again gathered into their own land, and into his church, and with them the fulness of the Gentiles. He *will* accomplish all his infinitely benevolent purposes of mercy and grace to this fallen world, in his own time, and by his own appointed means, — a preached gospel. He can and will make his word quick and powerful, and effectual to the salvation of thousands and millions of sinners. He can clothe his ministers with salvation, enrich them with all the gifts and graces of his Spirit, make sinners tremble under their faithful and powerful preaching, and saints shout aloud for joy. He can render the weap-

14*

ons of their warfare, with which his Spirit has furnished them, mighty and irresistible. All the strongholds of sin and Satan through the earth shall, in due time, fall before them. All kings shall serve him; all nations bow at his feet and worship him. Nothing shall be left to hurt or annoy in all his holy mountain. Peace shall come to Zion as a river, and righteousness as an overflowing stream. Satan, for a thousand years, shall be bound and shut up in the dark prison of hell, and the saints possess the kingdom, under the peaceful reign of Messiah, their Prince.

These, my brethren, are some of the great and glorious things foretold of Zion, the city of our God. They will all be accomplished in the millennium, which is certainly near at hand. Look, in the light of prophecy, on the present state of the world and the church. God has been shaking and overturning the nations in a manner unusually awful and terrible. Wars and desolations have prevailed, proud tyrants have been humbled in the dust, the power and influence of the man of sin reduced to a shadow, and the waters of the mystical Euphrates in a great measure dried up. A spirit of harmony pervades all denominations of Christians; their zeal is enkindled, and burns with increasing ardor. They are uniting their efforts to extend the Redeemer's kingdom. Already have their endeavors been crowned with very encouraging success in India, Africa, and other heathen countries. The Scriptures

have been translated into many languages, and sent
to nations who never before saw the Bible. Numerous societies for this purpose, and also for sending missionaries to the heathen nations around the
globe, have, within a few years, been formed in
Europe and America. God, who excited this spirit
of harmony and zeal in the breasts of Christians,
and prompted them to these measures, is giving us
the strongest intimations that he is about to usher
in the glories of the millennial day. Let us derive
fresh courage and resolution from these intimations
of his providence, as well as from the gracious and
highly encouraging promises in his word. The
work, my brethren, is the Lord's, but we may be
willing instruments in his hands. To this honor let
our hearts aspire. And to him be all the praise and
the glory of his great salvation forever. Amen.